PERILOUS

ABOUT THE AUTHOR

Janet Edwards lives in England and writes science fiction. As a child, she read everything she could get her hands on, including a huge amount of science fiction and fantasy. She studied Maths at Oxford, and went on to suffer years of writing unbearably complicated technical documents before deciding to write something that was fun for a change. She has a husband, a son, a lot of books, and an aversion to housework.

Visit Janet online at her website www.janetedwards.com to see the current list of her books. You can also make sure you don't miss future books by signing up to get an email alert when there's a new release.

ALSO BY JANET EDWARDS

Set in the Hive Future

PERILOUS: Hive Mind A Prequel Novella

TELEPATH

Set in the Game Future

REAPER

Set in the 25th century Portal Future

SCAVENGER ALLIANCE

Set in the 28th century Portal Future

The Earth Girl trilogy:-

EARTH GIRL

EARTH STAR

EARTH FLIGHT

Related stories :-

EARTH AND FIRE: An Earth Girl Novella

FRONTIER: An Epsilon Sector Novella

EARTH 2788: The Earth Girl Short Stories

HERA 2781: A Military Short Story

JANET EDWARDS

PERILOUS

HIVE MIND
A PREQUEL NOVELLA

To Theresa

This is where Amber's day begins

Janet Edwards

Copyright © Janet Edwards 2017

www.janetedwards.com

ISBN: 1976565456
ISBN-13: 978-1976565458

Janet Edwards asserts the moral right to be identified as the author of this work.

This novel is entirely a work of fiction. Names, characters, businesses, places, events and incidents are the products of the author's imagination or used in a fictitious manner. Any resemblance to actual persons, living or dead, or actual events or localities is purely coincidental.

All rights reserved. This book or any portion thereof may not be reproduced or used in any manner whatsoever without the express written permission of Janet Edwards except for the use of brief quotations in a book review.

Cover Design by The Cover Collection
Cover Design © Janet Edwards 2017

CHAPTER ONE

It was a week before Carnival, our Hive city's annual festival of light and life, when I tried cliff climbing for the first time and hit my head on the sky.

All twenty-two of the seventeen-year-olds living on my corridor had gone on a trip to Teen Level beach that day. The wind and wave machines were set for swimming rather than surfing, but only Forge and I were strong enough swimmers to venture into the deep water. Most of the others settled for paddling in the shallows, while my best friend, Shanna, preferred to stretch out lazily on the sand, basking in the warmth of the large sun-effect lights that shone dazzlingly bright on the blue painted ceiling.

Forge and I finally tired of swimming and headed to join Shanna. Forge threw himself down on the sand next to her, and gave her an enthusiastic hug and kiss, but she squealed in protest and pushed him away.

"You're horribly wet and cold."

Forge laughed, kissed her again, and she gave a resigned groan.

I sat down on the other side of Shanna, towelled my hair dry, and tugged an old tunic and leggings on over my wet swimming costume. It was early to be eating lunch, but swimming always made me hungry, so I rummaged in my bag for my sandwiches. I was happily munching them, while idly watching the gulls flying to and from their nests on the cliff-effect walls and structural pillars, when Forge turned to look at me.

"I think you should try cliff climbing, Amber."

I choked on my mouthful of sandwich. Shanna patted me on the back, passed me a bottle of water, and gave her boyfriend a withering look.

"That's a ridiculous suggestion. Amber fell out of a tree in her local park when she was six years old, broke her leg, and she's been terrified of heights ever since."

I'd been seven years old when I fell out of the tree, and I'd broken my arm not my leg, but I was too busy gulping down water to correct Shanna.

"I know Amber's terrified of heights," said Forge. "That's why I suggested she should try cliff climbing. I thought it would help her beat her fear."

By this time, I'd regained my powers of speech. I was tempted to tell Forge to go and waste himself, but he was my friend so I went for a polite reply instead. "I'm not keen on the idea."

"I didn't mean that you should try the advanced climbs that I do," said Forge. "I was thinking you could do the basic 'C' grade cliff climb."

"I'm still not keen on the idea."

"The 'C' grade climb is very simple." Forge gave me an encouraging smile. "You'd be wearing a harness and safety line, so you couldn't possibly fall."

I gnawed doubtfully at my bottom lip, and turned to stare at the cliffs. A girl who didn't look more than fourteen was completing a climb.

"You could just climb up a little way," added Forge, in coaxing tones. "If you do find you're scared, then you can come down again right away."

The girl had pulled herself up onto the ledge at the top of the climb, and was waving happily at the instructor. I saw how high up she was, pictured myself standing on the same ledge, and shuddered.

I turned back to face Forge, and opened my mouth to tell him that there was absolutely no way that I was going to try cliff climbing. "Only a very little way."

"Wonderful." Forge beamed at me.

I couldn't understand what had just happened. I'd intended to give Forge an absolute refusal, but instead I'd agreed to give cliff climbing a try. What should I do now? I'd look silly if I instantly announced I'd changed my mind. Perhaps wearing a harness and safety line would really make a difference. Perhaps the part of my mind that was terrified of heights would realize I couldn't fall and not be scared at all. Perhaps there was truly a chance that making the climb would cure my fear.

Five minutes later, the cliff climbing instructor was buckling me into a harness, and attaching my safety line. "If you get stuck at any point, then give me a shout, and I'll lower you down. All right, Amber?"

I was too nervous to speak, so I grunted a response and headed for the cliff. I'd watched Forge doing the complex advanced climbs dozens of times. This one should be perfectly simple.

To my surprise it *was* perfectly simple. I moved easily up the mass of pegs hammered into the side of the cliff, and was almost enjoying myself until I heard Forge shouting encouragement at me. I made the mistake of looking down, and saw him standing next to Shanna. The two figures, one dark-haired and muscular, the other blonde and slender, seemed a dizzying distance below me.

I hastily turned my gaze upwards again, focusing on the textured, concrete surface of the cliff, and the sight of my own hands clenched tightly on the climbing pegs. I told myself that I was being ridiculous. There was only one beach on each level of our Hive because they were made on such a vast scale. They covered a huge area, and their ceilings were far higher than those in the shopping areas or even the parks, but I still couldn't be much more than three times the height of a standard room ceiling off the ground.

"Are you all right, Amber?" called the climbing instructor.

I was far from all right. My head had gone from thinking about the height of a park ceiling to remembering the day I broke my arm. I'd climbed a tree in the neighbourhood park, because I wanted to write my name on the ceiling, but a branch broke under my weight. There'd been an instant of pure terror as I tumbled downwards, followed by agonizing pain as I hit the ground and broke my arm.

A fall from this cliff would be far worse. I tried reminding myself that I was wearing a harness attached to a safety line, but that made no difference. There was a terrifying sheer drop beneath me, the pegs under my hands seemed to shrink in size, and the safety line holding me felt like a fragile thread of cotton.

A mocking yell came from below. "Amber's got stuck on the cliff. Coward!"

That was Reece's voice. What was he doing down there? I'd thought he was safely occupied leering at the girl swimmers in their skimpy costumes.

A female voice snapped at him. "Shut up, Reece!"

"Yes, be quiet," said a male voice.

Those voices belonged to Margot and Atticus. Our whole corridor group must have come over to watch me do this climb. If I didn't make it to the top, I'd look a fool in front of all of them, and Reece would keep taunting me about it for the whole of our remaining year on Teen Level.

I had to make it to the top of this climb. I took a deep breath, forced my right hand to release its grip on one peg, and grabbed at the next. I was still horribly aware of my height above the ground, so I closed my eyes before attempting to move either of my feet.

It was ridiculous, but I felt far better climbing with my eyes shut. Now there was no terrifying drop beneath me, just comforting darkness, the sound of gulls screeching, the taste of salt on the breeze, and the warm feel of the pegs under my hands and feet.

I must surely be getting close to the top of the climb. I groped my way further upwards, expecting to feel the edge of the ledge under my hands at any moment, but instead I thumped my head against the unyielding, painted sky.

I yelped in pain, and a wave of dizziness swept over me. I lost my self-control entirely, and clung to my handholds with the death grip of panic.

"Amber, the ledge is an arm's length to your right," Forge called from below.

I was too shocked to answer him. There were stabbing pains in my head, and something was trickling down my face. I wanted to rub the wetness away with a hand, but daren't let go of the pegs I was holding.

The trickle reached my mouth, I tasted blood, and realized I'd cut my head on one of the light fittings in the ceiling. I didn't think there were any of the big sun-effect lights near the edge of the sky, so it was probably one of the multitude of tinier lights that were there for the stars effect at night.

I still had my eyes closed, and I wasn't moving, but I felt a weird spinning sensation. Forge was calling to me again, but his voice seemed distant and irrelevant. The only things that mattered now were the handholds and footholds that kept me from plummeting downwards.

"Coward!" yelled Reece again.

"Shut up!" shouted Forge and the climbing instructor in unison. The female voice of the climbing instructor continued solo. "I can see you've hurt your head, Amber. Let go of the handholds, and I'll lower you down on your safety line."

My brain didn't seem to be working properly, so it took me a moment to make sense of her words, but then I felt an instinctive terror at the thought of letting go. I could dimly hear Forge talking to the climbing instructor.

"Amber's in real trouble up there."

"I'll go up after her," said the climbing instructor.

"It's better if I go. She knows me." Forge's voice suddenly got a lot louder. "Hold on, Amber! I just need a moment to sort out a harness and safety line, and then I'll come up and help you."

Forge was coming to help me. I clung to the cliff like a desperate human spider. It was only a moment, it was only a century, before I heard Forge's voice coming from beside me.

"Amber, you're going to climb slowly down the cliff, with me guiding your hands and feet. Do you understand?"

He paused for a moment, waiting for me to reply. I managed a terrified squeak.

"I'm going to move your right foot first. Try to relax and trust me, Amber."

I felt Forge's hand take my foot. I did my best to follow his orders, and not resist when he moved it away from one peg and down to rest on another. He moved my right hand next, talked me into moving my left foot, and then my left hand.

There was another yell from Reece. "It's going to take weeks to get the baby down like that. You should just unclip her harness and push her off the cliff. That'll get her down a lot faster and... Ow, that hurt!"

"Who hit Reece?" shouted Forge.

Shanna's voice called back. "Atticus, Margot, and me."

"Good job," said Forge. "If Reece says one more word, hit him again."

"If Reece says one more word, I'm calling Health and Safety to arrest him." The climbing instructor sounded furious.

Forge's voice started murmuring encouragement again. I tried to forget my height above the ground, and that my entire social circle was watching me make a fool of myself, and concentrated on following his instructions. I inched my way down at a snail's pace, counting each time I moved my feet down to a fresh foothold.

Ten minutes later, I felt the sand of the beach beneath my feet. I blinked blood from my eyes, and glanced downwards to check I really was standing safely on the ground, before letting go of my handholds.

"Well done, Amber." Forge unclipped both our safety lines.

I unbuckled my harness, slipped it off, and looked back up at the cliff. The ledge at the top was impossible to miss if a climber stayed on the correct route. I must have drifted sideways when I was climbing with my eyes closed.

"Amber, you're covered in blood," said Shanna.

I thought she was exaggerating, but I touched my hair with my right hand, and found it was startlingly wet and sticky.

"I bumped my head on one of the stars in the ceiling," I said.

Shanna advanced on Forge and glowered at him. "This is all your fault. You shouldn't have forced poor Amber into climbing that cliff."

Forge was much taller than his girlfriend, and bulky with the muscles of a competition standard swimmer and surfer, but he backed off a nervous step or two. "I didn't *force* Amber into climbing the cliff. I just *suggested* she should climb the cliff."

I wasn't sure if it was the bump on my head, or the sight of the blood on my right hand, but the spinning sensation started again, and the lights in the ceiling seemed to be flickering on and off. I hurriedly sat down on the sand.

Atticus came to kneel beside me and peered at my head. "I suggest we stop arguing and focus on helping Amber."

The climbing instructor pushed her way through the crowd, and looked down at me. "I've called Hive Emergency Services, Amber. A paramedic is on the way to treat you."

"I don't need a paramedic to treat me," I said. "I only bumped my head."

"You do need a paramedic to treat you. You have a significant head injury." The climbing instructor turned to Reece. "What's your identity code, Reece?"

"My identity code?" Reece took a step backwards. "You don't need to know my identity code. I don't want to register to try cliff climbing."

"I had an injured climber in difficulties at the top of the cliff, and you deliberately disrupted attempts to assist her. I'm reporting you to Health and Safety for criminal endangerment."

"You mustn't do that," Reece's voice held an edge of panic now. "I've been reported twice in the last six months, and had hasties come to my room and lecture me. If I get reported again, I'll get a telepath squad turning up at my door. I don't want one of those creepy telepaths nosing round in my thoughts."

"Telling me that you've got a history of bad behaviour just confirms I'm correct in deciding to report you," said the climbing instructor. "What's your identity code?"

Reece turned, shoved his way between Margot and Preeja, and ran off down the beach. The climbing instructor looked after him with a frown and turned to Forge. "What's Reece's identity code?"

Forge hesitated before speaking. "I don't know."

"Where is his room then?"

"I don't know that either."

The climbing instructor sighed. "I can't believe that, Forge. You obviously know the boy very well."

I was shocked when Margot joined the conversation. "Reece lives on the same corridor as the rest of us. His identity code is 2514-0217-811."

"Thank you." The climbing instructor tapped the code into her dataview, picked up my discarded harness, and headed back towards the cliff.

"Reece is going to get in massive trouble over this," said Margot, in a voice of malicious satisfaction. "Three reports within twelve months. Four if the climbing instructor reports him for both criminal endangerment and refusing to identify himself."

"You didn't have to volunteer Reece's identity code like that," said Forge.

"Yes, I did," said Margot. "The climbing instructor has already got the identity codes for both you and Amber from your cliff climbing registrations. If we refused to tell her how to find Reece, then Health and Safety could just send a telepath squad after you two instead. Do you want a telepath squad knocking at your door, Forge? Would you enjoy having a nosy dig through your mind to find information about Reece? I know Amber wouldn't."

I had an instant sickening image of me opening my door, and finding one of the hideous grey-clad telepaths standing there, with their escort of four blue-uniformed hasties. I feared nosies as much as I feared heights, so I rushed to support Margot.

"You did the right thing, Margot."

"I don't feel any obligation to protect Reece anyway." Margot's voice was bitter now. "Remember the last time he was reported? I'd caught him painting insults on my room door. I'm sick of his behaviour, and I vote we exclude him from our corridor group for Carnival."

"Excluding someone isn't just bad for the person that's left isolated and alone," said Forge, "but can cause divisions in the corridor group too. We don't want to turn into one of those corridors with two or three rival groups that are constantly arguing over who gets to use the corridor community room."

"There's no danger of that happening to us over Reece," said Margot. "Nobody is going to take his side against the exclusion, because nobody likes him."

Forge still looked doubtful. "Even if our whole corridor group is united in the decision, excluding someone for Carnival is a big penalty. Reece would be left on his own at all the parties."

Preeja joined in the argument. "There's no rule saying you can only socialize with the teens on your own corridor. Reece could go and annoy some of the other seventeen-year-olds for a change."

"After four years living on Teen Level, the other seventeen-year-olds all have their established friends," said Forge. "They won't want Reece bothering them."

Atticus got back to his feet. "Reece deserves to be left on his own for Carnival. We've warned him about his behaviour over and over again. Every time he's promised to reform but is acting just as repellently within days. Linnette and I caught him teasing Casper only yesterday evening."

There was stunned silence at the uncharacteristic outburst from quiet, thoughtful Atticus.

"I don't understand why you're all turning against Reece," said Forge. "I know he went too far painting insults on Margot's door, and he shouldn't have made fun of Amber when she was stuck on the cliff, but he behaves himself most of the time."

"Reece is a loathsome bully," said Margot. "You don't realize how bad he is, Forge, because he never picks on you or Shanna. Reece is smart enough to attack easier targets. People like Casper. People like Linnette. People like me!"

"Margot's right," said Linnette. "Half a dozen of us went shopping yesterday, and Casper accidentally bumped into a display cabinet in one of the shops. An ornament fell off a shelf and got broken. Casper was distraught about it, but the shopkeeper was very understanding."

"He was nice," said Casper, smiling happily.

"We sorted everything out," continued Linnette, "and Casper

calmed down again, but that evening Atticus and I caught Reece frightening him. He was telling Casper that he was useless, nobody liked him, and he was going to be thrown out of the Hive for breaking things."

Casper's face crumpled into distress. "I don't want to be sent Outside to be attacked by the hunter of souls. I don't want to be traded to another Hive either. I want to stay here."

Linnette patted his arm. "What Reece told you was wrong, Casper. You're very helpful, we all like you, and nobody is going to throw you out of the Hive."

Casper brightened up again.

"I'd no idea that Reece had sunk to the depths of upsetting Casper," said Forge, with an angry edge to his voice. "Well, you've convinced me that we need to take action. Who votes in favour of excluding Reece for Carnival?"

A host of hands shot up, including mine. Forge raised his own hand and did some solemn counting. "Twenty in favour. Are you abstaining, Casper?"

Casper gave him an uncertain look.

"Are you voting in favour?" asked Forge.

Casper shook his head.

"Are you voting against?"

Casper hesitated for a moment, and then shook his head again.

"All right," said Forge. "Casper is abstaining from voting because he's far too kind to vote to exclude anyone, however mean they are to him, so effectively that's a unanimous decision. Reece is excluded until after the three days of Carnival celebrations. We don't invite him to our parties. We don't allow him in the corridor community room. We don't talk to him. We don't even acknowledge he exists."

"The paramedic is coming now." Shanna pointed at where a man was walking across the beach towards us. He was wearing the dramatic red and blue, diagonal striped uniform of Emergency Services, and had what looked like a chunky-wheeled stretcher chasing after him.

Everyone watched in silence as the paramedic knelt beside

me. He tapped the white name badge on his shoulder. "I'm Barnard, and I've come to treat your injury. What is your name and identity code?"

"Amber 2514-0172-912," I recited.

"Hello Amber." He took a dataview from his pocket, tapped it to make it unfurl, and entered the code. "You're seventeen, and live in Blue Zone, area 510/6120, corridor 11, room 6?"

"That's right."

"I was told that you injured your head climbing the cliff, Amber. Did you fall off?"

"No, I just bumped my head on the ceiling. There's a slight cut, but it's nothing to worry about."

"Please lie down, Amber."

I lay back on the sand. Barnard peered at my head, waved what looked like a mini scanner at it, and then scribbled my name on a white plastic bracelet and attached it to my wrist. I turned my head to study it, reminded of the tracking bracelets children had to wear until they were ten years old.

"Is your head hurting, Amber?"

"A bit."

"I'll give you some mild pain killers."

He handed me two virulently purple tablets. I dutifully chewed and swallowed them.

"I'm taking you to a medical facility now," said Barnard. "Once you've had an initial examination from one of their doctors, you'll probably be given some stronger pain relief."

"But I don't need to go to a medical facility. It's only a little cut."

He ignored my protest, and brought the wheeled stretcher alongside me. I looked at it nervously, and was about to ask if I was supposed to climb onto it, when something slid out of the side and scooped me aboard.

"Please lift up your arms, Amber."

I lifted my arms. Barnard fastened one strap across my chest, another across my legs, and started the stretcher moving. Despite the straps holding me in place, I grabbed at the sides of the stretcher to make sure I couldn't fall off.

"Can one of us go to the medical facility with Amber?" asked Forge.

"I'm afraid that isn't possible," said Barnard. "Teen Level Cascade Triage is in operation."

"What does that mean?" I asked.

"It means that all the Teen Level medical facilities are overloaded, so each case has to be assessed, and some may be sent to more distant medical facilities."

"Why are…?"

My words were drowned out by a siren sounding, followed by a deafening voice from overhead speakers. "Swimmer in distress! Clear the way for beach rescue!"

CHAPTER TWO

My stretcher jerked to a halt, and two men carrying flotation devices sprinted past us, heading towards the water.

"Waste it, not another one!" snapped Barnard. "Amber, wait here for me."

He ran off, and everyone else followed him. I was left alone, strapped to my wheeled stretcher. No, not totally alone. Atticus was still standing next to me, looking down at me with a frown.

"Margot seems determined to get Reece into trouble," I said.

"I don't blame her. Did you see what he painted on her door?"

"No. Forge and I were at swimming training that afternoon, and someone from Accommodation Services had cleaned the paint off before we got back."

"Well, I heard Margot crying, and went to help her, so I saw there was a savagely nasty mention of her sister. I didn't understand what it was about, but Margot was completely incoherent with distress, and I had to call Accommodation Services on her behalf."

I grimaced. I'd thought only Preeja and I knew the secret about Margot's older sister. Even Shanna and Linnette hadn't been told, because Margot had been worried that Shanna would react by saying something tactless, while Linnette had been away attending an advanced course in the care of nocturnal creatures during the crucial couple of weeks.

I was sure that neither Preeja nor Margot would have trusted

Reece with the secret, so he must have found out about it by sneaking around and listening at doors. If he'd been tormenting Margot about her sister, then I wasn't surprised that she was trying to get him in trouble.

Atticus waved a dismissive hand. "Forget about Reece. Why did you try climbing that cliff, Amber? I couldn't believe it when I saw you up there. You must have known that you'd get into difficulties. You get frightened just standing on a stepladder to hang decorations on a park tree."

I sighed. "Forge suggested that climbing the cliff would help me conquer my fear of heights. It seemed worth a try. I didn't think I'd be so scared when I had a safety line to stop me from falling."

"I admire you for trying to beat your fear, but I suggest you don't do it again."

"I won't." I changed the subject. "What did the paramedic mean about all the Teen Level medical facilities being overloaded? They didn't seem busy when I went for my last annual medical check."

"They'll be busy now because we're getting close to the Carnival celebrations, and you know what happens after those finish," said Atticus, in a startlingly grim voice.

"The Lottery of 2531."

"Exactly. In ten days' time, every eighteen-year-old in our Hive will be saying final farewells to their teen friends, and then heading for their assessment centres. They know they'll be hit with a barrage of tests that will decide their whole future life. They're naturally going to be nervous about that, and in some cases the nerves will turn into outright panic."

I recited the words that were on the wall of every community centre on Teen Level. "The five years on Teen Level climax in the thrilling week of Lottery. Eighteen-year-olds are assessed, allocated, optimized and imprinted, emerging from Lottery as proudly productive adult members of the Hive."

I wrinkled my nose. "I can understand the eighteen-year-olds being nervous though. Teen Level 50 is halfway up the Hive. Everyone wants to do well in Lottery, and be assigned to a higher level of the Hive, but realistically half of us will end up going down to lower levels."

"Our chances are much worse than that," said Atticus. "When I was a child in school, the teachers kept saying there were a hundred million people and a hundred accommodation levels in the Hive. That made it sound as if there were a million people living on each accommodation level."

He paused. "That's not true though. There are just pipes and waste systems down on Level 100, so the Hive only has ninety-nine real accommodation levels. There must be about five million of us packed into Teen Level, which works because we have one small room each. Adults all have apartments though, and everyone knows that higher level people have bigger apartments."

He pulled a face. "If you think about it logically, that means there must be far fewer people living in luxury on Level 1 than those living in cramped apartments on Level 99. There are twenty-two of us living on our corridor. My guess is that only seven or eight of us will be heading up the Hive after we go through Lottery, while the rest will go down."

I frowned. I'd worked these things out for myself as a child in school, and kept quiet about them because a loyal member of the Hive didn't question what the teachers told her. It was disconcerting to hear the quiet Atticus openly say something so rebellious.

Atticus shrugged. "The idea of going down the Hive doesn't worry me though. My parents are Level 80, so I've never had any great expectations about what Lottery will assign me."

I was disconcerted again. Teen Level equality rules said that you never told the other teens what level your parents were. When you went to visit your family, you made sure you were alone in the lift so no one would see your destination level. I'd known a few teens, including Reece, break that rule to smugly point out their parents were among the elite who lived in the top ten accommodation levels of the Hive.

Such attempts at showing off were always met with the hostile response that your parents' level didn't matter any longer, because all teens were Level 50 and equal. I'd never known anyone admit to having low level parents, so I'd no idea how to reply.

"My parents may only be Level 80, and doing simple work caring for plants in hydroponics, but they're happy," continued Atticus. "They're proud to be doing something as important as feeding the Hive."

I finally found something safe to say. "Feeding the Hive is vital work."

Atticus nodded. "Even if I end up on Level 99, I know I'll be doing useful work. I'll have an apartment of my own rather than a single room, and a better income than the pathetic teen living allowance. My theory is that the Hive sets things up that way deliberately. Teens from high level families must find the transition to the minimal lifestyle on Teen Level hard to start with, but it means that everyone's living standards improve when they come out of Lottery."

I knew that Atticus was right about teens from high level families finding it hard to adjust to Teen Level. When I first arrived on Teen Level as a thirteen-year-old, I'd thought my room horribly small compared to my old bedroom in my parents' Level 27 apartment, and struggled to buy what I considered necessities on my miserly living allowance.

I was less sure about everyone's living standards improving when they came out of Lottery. I'd heard plenty of jokes about how Level 99 Sewage Technicians lived in hovels among the pipes, and assumed people were exaggerating the poor conditions, but I'd no actual knowledge of what life was like down there.

"What frightens me about Lottery isn't the uncertainty of what level I'll be afterwards," said Atticus, "but the fact I'll have my brain imprinted with the information required to do my work."

"But being imprinted will be wonderful," I said. "We'll be given the gift of a wealth of knowledge."

"That's what everyone tells us," said Atticus cynically, "and it's what we all obediently repeat, but I find the idea of someone messing with my brain quite terrifying. Haven't you thought about that, Amber?"

I hadn't thought about the imprinting process before – my worries about Lottery had always been focused on whether I'd be rated high or low level – but I was thinking about it now. Was imprinting painful, and did having all that extra knowledge change your personality?

Forge and Shanna came back to join us, with all the rest of our corridor group except Reece trailing after them.

"Did beach rescue save the swimmer in distress?" I asked.

"Yes," said Forge eagerly. "Beach rescue were amazing. I'm one of the best swimmers in the Blue Zone teen swimming team. Maybe when I go through Lottery, I'll be assigned to beach rescue myself."

"You should want Lottery to assign you to either the Blue Zone adult swimming team or the surfing team," said Shanna reprovingly. "A professional athlete is far higher level than a mere beach rescuer."

"Being high level and swimming for my home zone would be nice, but there'd be more satisfaction in rescuing distressed swimmers." Forge sighed. "Well, Lottery will decide my future, not me. I just hope..."

He broke off because the paramedic had returned. "I'll take you to a medical facility for treatment now, Amber," said Barnard.

My stretcher started moving off across the sand again. "We'll see you later," called Shanna.

I lifted a hand in acknowledgement. My stretcher jolted across the sands, the motion sending a jarring pain through my head, but then we went through some double doors. The distant, blue beach sky, with its dazzlingly bright suns, was replaced by a standard-height white ceiling with ordinary lighting, and my stretcher rolled smoothly along a corridor.

There was only one beach on each level of the Hive, so they were always near the area 500/5000 centre point, and had major belt interchanges at every entrance so people from distant areas of the Hive could travel there as quickly as possible. I expected us to stop at the interchange by this beach entrance, and was wondering what it would be like to ride the belt system strapped to this stretcher, but we kept going on along the corridor to a row of express lifts.

Barnard pressed the button to summon a lift. "Your head injury appears to be minor, Amber, so Teen Level Cascade Triage has given you a low crisis rating and is sending you to another level of the Hive for treatment."

I was being sent to another level of the Hive for treatment! I knew it was ridiculous to feel nervous about that, but I'd lived with my parents on Level 27 until I was thirteen years old and moved to live on Teen Level 50.

I'd gone for lots of rides on the upways and downways since then, usually illegally balancing on the handrail until blue-uniformed hasties intervened and scolded me. On each of those rides, I'd peered nosily at the other levels as the moving stairs carried me past them, but I'd never actually set foot on any of them.

A well-behaved member of the Hive stayed on their home level, only going to other levels when their work required it or to visit close relatives. Once a week, I visited my parents on Level 27. My age and clothes made me conspicuous, so every hasty who saw me would check my identity and make sure I wasn't straying from the direct route to my parents' apartment.

I told myself that I couldn't get in trouble for going to another level to have my injury treated, but that didn't make me feel any better. I was feeling vulnerable and wanted to stay on familiar territory.

"You'll be treated at a Level 93 medical facility," continued Barnard.

"Level 93?" I repeated anxiously. "But that's almost at the bottom of the Hive!"

"Don't worry about that. You'll still receive medical treatment of a high standard."

The doors of one of the lifts opened, and Barnard guided my stretcher inside. A moment later, I was watching the numbers change rapidly on the lift level indicator. The lift stopped at Level 63, and the doors opened to show a group of men wearing maintenance uniforms. They took one look at me lying on my stretcher, face smeared in blood, and stepped backwards.

"You go ahead," said one of them.

The doors closed again, and the lift moved on down, stopping again at Level 69. This time the doors opened to show four men and women in the blue uniforms of Health and Safety, and a female grey-clad figure wearing an oddly shaped mask that enveloped her whole head.

I gasped in shock. A telepath squad! Was this something to do with the climbing instructor reporting Reece to Health and Safety, or just a random encounter? Telepath squads roamed everywhere in the Hive, reading minds to check for criminal thoughts, so it could just be pure chance that one had stopped our lift.

I waited tensely, hoping the telepath squad would do the same as the maintenance workers, and back away to let our lift continue without them, but they stepped inside. The lift doors closed, and the telepath moved to stand by my stretcher and look down at me. I saw the purple glint of inhuman eyes studying me from within her bulging grey mask.

The telepath spoke in a weird, throbbing voice. "There's no need to be afraid, Amber."

CHAPTER THREE

The telepath knew my name and that I was scared! Well, of course the telepath would know those things. People called the telepaths nosies because they nosed around in your thoughts, prying through all your secrets, and this nosy was reading my mind right now.

"You're injured, but you will get medical treatment very soon, Amber," said the nosy. "You're nervous of my presence, but I am here to protect you and all loyal members of the Hive."

I didn't say anything. I couldn't speak. I couldn't even breathe. I'd seen telepath squads hundreds of times before when I was travelling through the Hive. Whenever possible, I'd changed my route to escape them. Sometimes I'd been unlucky enough to be riding on the belt system or the moving stairs and be carried close by one of them. There'd been a few occasions when I'd been waiting for a lift, the doors had opened, I'd seen a telepath squad already inside it, and practically run away in terror.

There'd only been one occasion when I was in a lift and a telepath squad entered it. I'd thought it was the ultimate horror when I had to brush close past the nosy to escape through the open lift doors, but this was far worse. I was strapped down on a stretcher, powerless to escape, with the nosy looking down at me and studying my thoughts.

I was deeply relieved when the nosy turned away from me and looked at Barnard instead. "Only criminals and those who plan to harm others have any reason to fear telepaths," she said.

Barnard instantly took two steps backwards and collided with the lift wall. I thought he was just suffering from the same horror of nosies as me, but then he started gabbling defensively.

"I admit I'm angry about my girlfriend dumping me, but that's natural in the circumstances. I may have gone as far as imagining doing a few things to her and her new boyfriend, but that was nothing more than fantasy."

The nosy studied Barnard for a moment before speaking. "This has already gone further than imagination."

"I called her a couple of times," said Barnard. "Pushed a note or two under her door. I wouldn't have hurt either of them though. I *won't* hurt either of them."

"It's true that you won't hurt either of them," said the nosy. "You won't be allowed to harm anyone now that I've seen the images in your mind. I know what you've already done and what you planned to do in the future. You are now under arrest for intention to injure others."

"You don't need to arrest me," said Barnard. "I won't go anywhere near either of them. Not ever again. I promise."

"We will accompany you while you take Amber to the medical facility for treatment," said the nosy. "We will then escort you to a Health and Safety Unit for a full assessment and a decision on appropriate corrective treatment."

There was dead silence until the lift doors opened again on Level 93, and we moved out into a corridor. I held on to the sides of my stretcher, my knuckles white with tension. How far would we have to travel to reach the medical facility? How long would I have to endure a grey-clad nosy prying through my thoughts?

I told myself the nosy wasn't interested in me. She'd obviously caught Barnard thinking of harming his ex-girlfriend, and brought her squad into the lift to intercept him. The nosy would surely have her attention focused on Barnard's mind, not mine, but I still tried to think dutiful thoughts.

It was good that the telepaths patrolled our Hive, preventing people like Barnard from hurting anyone. It was good that they stopped anyone from stealing property or damaging the Hive. It was good that I could go anywhere I wanted in total safety.

Naturally the telepaths had to read the minds of innocent people like me as part of the process of preventing criminals from committing crimes. That was unfortunate, but I was sure they kept such intrusions to the bare minimum.

I wasn't convincing myself, so I doubted I was convincing the nosy, but she didn't say a word as we headed along a corridor lined with apartment doors. I noticed the distance between those doors was far smaller than between the doors of apartments where my parents lived on Level 27. My parents lived on a corridor with family sized apartments though, and these might be the apartments of single people.

A door ahead of us opened, a laughing man stepped out, and the nosy stopped and turned to gaze at him in silence. The man's laughter broke off, his face registered alarm, and he scurried back into his apartment. The nosy started walking again, and we moved on to where the corridor ended in an open area. There were the entrances to two more corridors, some wall murals showing park scenes, and double doors marked with the red symbol of a medical facility.

We went through the doors into a reception area. Uniformed medical staff, and a scattering of waiting people who must be other patients, all turned to look at the telepath squad in horror. The nosy said nothing, just turned and walked out of the door again, followed by the hasties and Barnard.

The receptionist came hurrying over to me. "Why did that telepath squad come in here?"

"They came to arrest the paramedic because he was planning to hurt someone. They let him bring me here before they took him away for corrective treatment."

"Oh." The receptionist stared across at the double doors. "I wonder if I need to tell anyone about the paramedic being arrested, or if the telepath squad will do that?"

"I don't know, and I don't care." I'd forced myself to lie still on my stretcher in the presence of the telepath, but now I lost control. I started tugging at the strap across my chest, trying to free myself.

"Please don't do that," said the receptionist. "I understand you've had a stressful time, and I promise we'll get you off the stretcher in just a moment."

She peered at the bracelet on my wrist. "Amber 2514-0172-912. Yes, we've been expecting your arrival."

She waved her arm, and a woman in white overalls towed my stretcher down the corridor to a small room labelled "Treatment 4". The stretcher lined up beside the single white bed, the woman undid the straps imprisoning me, and the stretcher slid me neatly across onto the bed.

"A doctor will be with you shortly." The woman went out of the door, taking the stretcher with her.

I was free from the straps. The telepath squad must be far away by now. The tablets I'd been given had stopped my head hurting. I closed my eyes, and tried to relax, but couldn't. The feel of a solid bed under me, rather than a proper sleep field, was an unpleasant reminder that I wasn't in my own room but in a strange place on Level 93.

Why had I been sent to Level 93 for treatment? Was it a warning omen for my future Lottery result? Forge was an accomplished athlete, and Shanna could make startlingly creative clothes from the cheapest possible materials, but I'd tried all the activity sessions offered at our nearest community centre without discovering I had a talent for any of them. The only time I'd been given one of the coveted gold cards that entitled someone to attend advanced sessions in an activity was for my swimming, and I knew I didn't have the height or build for Lottery to make me a professional swimmer.

The harsh truth was that Lottery would be sending Forge and Shanna up the Hive – they might even end up in the elite top ten levels – while I'd be going down. People said I was reasonably bright, so there was still hope I'd be assigned to something like Level 60 work, but I should face the fact I could end up here on Level 93.

I opened my eyes again and studied the room. The white walls were a little battered, the ceiling was cracked, and the overhead scanning grid looked like an elderly model, but it was still better than the average medical room on Teen Level. The patients in the waiting room had been cheaply dressed, but again their clothes were better than my own tunic and leggings.

I remembered Atticus's comment about how everyone's living standards would improve when they came out of Lottery. What I'd seen so far on Level 93 seemed to confirm that was true. The hardest thing about coming out of Lottery as a Level 93 worker wouldn't be my living conditions, but knowing I'd be a disappointment to my mother and father.

I knew that I'd never see any of my teen friends again after Lottery. Its verdicts would divide us forever, scattering us across the hundred accommodation levels of the Hive. We'd been taught to accept that final break rather than struggle to keep friendships going against the barrier of a five, ten or even fifty level division.

Family ties were different. The Hive accepted there was a deep bond between parents and children. Whenever I got worried about the sharp transition that lay ahead for me at eighteen, the total change in lifestyle and the loss of all my friends, I comforted myself with the knowledge that I'd still have the support of my parents.

Now I was hit with a sickening thought. The Hive encouraged the maintenance of the bond between parents and children across level divisions, but some parents still chose to disown a child who came out of Lottery at an embarrassingly low level. I didn't think that mine would do that, but…

I was grateful for the distraction of the door opening. I lifted myself on one elbow, and saw an elderly man in a doctor's uniform. He smiled at me, but waved a reproving finger.

"Please lie down, Amber. A head injury can cause dizziness, even make you faint without warning, and I don't like my patients falling on the floor."

I lay back on the bed.

He studied his dataview and murmured to himself. "Recurrent headaches. Flagged as an allergy risk."

He came over and peered at my head. "Your admission record says that you were climbing the cliff on Teen Level beach and hit your head on a star. I've seen plenty of head injuries before, but never one from a star. Didn't you realize you were at the top of the climb?"

"I had my eyes closed during the climb because I'm scared of heights." I paused. "I suppose that sounds a bit strange."

"I've heard far stranger things." He turned on the scanning grid, moved its bar to above my head, and studied the wall display. "You don't seem to have done any serious damage to yourself, but I'd advise keeping your eyes open next time you climb a cliff."

I shuddered. "I'm never going cliff climbing again."

The doctor turned off the scanning grid, went across to a shelf, picked up a plastic pack, and ripped it open. "Head injuries always bleed a lot. I'll clean away the blood so I can see the cut."

He worked on my head with what felt like a wet cloth, and then sprayed the top of my head with icy liquid from a bottle. "The good news is the gash is well inside your hairline, so there's no risk of it leaving a visible scar," he said cheerfully. "The bad news is that the gash is well inside your hairline, so the glue will mess up your hair for a few days."

I was startled. "Glue?"

"Centuries ago, a doctor would have shaved part of your hair and stitched the wound. These days, we use a very special glue to seal the wound instead." He fetched another bottle from the shelf. "I've sprayed the wound area with skin absorbent local anaesthetic, but you may feel minor discomfort as I close the edges of the cut. Please try not to move for the next couple of minutes, and keep your eyes closed in case the glue spray drifts off target."

I closed my eyes, and braced myself to endure some pain, but there was just a slight tugging sensation.

"All done," said the doctor. "You can try sitting up now."

I sat up slowly, and swung my legs round to sit on the edge of the bed.

"Any dizziness?"

"No."

"Good. You'll find the top of your head feels numb for the next hour. Once the local anaesthetic wears off, you'll probably find your head starts hurting again, but I'll prescribe you pain killers to help with that."

He tapped busily at his dataview, and then looked at me again. "There's what will feel like, and effectively is, a solid lump of glue on your scalp. You can wash your hair as usual, but don't colour, comb, brush, or yank at that area of hair, and try not to bump your head again. The glue will vanish naturally in about ten days, after which you can go back to normal."

I touched the top of my head with a cautious finger. He was right. It did feel like a lump of glue was stuck in my hair. "Is it safe for me to go swimming?"

The doctor made a clicking sound with his tongue. "I think you should stay away from the wet sand on Teen Level beach for the next ten days, but a swimming pool should be safe enough."

"Thank you."

"I think we'll be keeping you in overnight," he added, "but you should be able to go back to Teen Level first thing in the morning."

I frowned. "Can't I go back to Teen Level now? My head feels perfectly fine."

"We need to make some further checks before we send you back to Teen Level. Someone will come along shortly and show you to another room. Goodbye, Amber."

The doctor wandered out of the room. I took my folded dataview from my pocket, tapped it to make it unfurl, and called Shanna. It was a moment before her face appeared on the dataview screen.

"Amber, are you all right? Where are you?"

"I'm in a medical facility on Level 93."

"Level 93!" Shanna shrieked in horror. "What are you doing down there? Do they even have doctors on Level 93?"

"A very nice doctor has treated me. Can you please tell the others that the doctor says I have to stay here overnight, but I'll see you all in the morning?"

"I expect they'll give you reject protein scum to eat," said Shanna gloomily.

Shanna was my best friend, but I was beginning to think I

should have called Preeja or Margot instead. "I have to go now. They're moving me to another room."

"I doubt the water on Level 93 is safe to drink either," said Shanna. "It must be horribly close to the sewage reclamation systems on Level 100."

"I've really got to go. See you tomorrow, Shanna."

I tapped my dataview to end the call, and pulled a face at the wall. Shanna had been my best friend since the day I arrived on Teen Level. My parents had delivered me to my bare, unwelcoming room, helped me unpack my set of basic clothes and possessions authorized under the Teen Level equality rules, made encouraging noises and left. I'd sat there for a while, feeling abandoned and desolate, before venturing out to find the corridor community room.

I'd never forget the moment when I walked in the door, and an intimidating crowd of strange thirteen-year-olds turned to look at me. I'd been on the brink of turning and running away, when Shanna stepped forward, gave me a smile that oozed self-confidence, and swept me into the conversation going on between her and another girl.

I'd still no idea what made Shanna choose me to be her best friend that day, rather than Margot, Linnette, Preeja, or one of the other half a dozen girls on our corridor. From the very beginning, it was obvious that beautiful Shanna and athletic Forge would pair off and be the joint leaders of our corridor group. Left to my own devices, I'd have hovered shyly on the fringes of that group, but as Shanna's best friend I was in the heart of all the activities and parties.

I was deeply grateful for that, and appreciative of all Shanna's good points, but I wasn't blind to her flaws. Shanna could be generous and supportive, but also demanded to be the centre of attention all the time, and sometimes said hurtful things without thinking. That call had been typical of her, enjoying herself shrieking about the food and water not being safe on Level 93, without considering how her words would affect me.

I tapped at my dataview again to check my messages. There were a dozen messages of good wishes from friends including

Atticus and Linnette, a public service reminder about the three-monthly test closure of the Hive bulkhead doors, and the daily summary of the Blue Zone sports results.

The door opened. I'd been expecting someone in a medical uniform to come and fetch me, but this was a girl wearing a cheap red top and skirt. Her hair was a mass of thick black curls, which clustered tightly round her dark face, and she looked so young that I could have believed she was seventeen like me. Her appearance had to be misleading though. If the girl was working here, then she must have gone through Lottery already and be at least nineteen.

"Hi, Amber." She grinned at me. "I'm Simone, but everyone calls me Buzz."

I couldn't help grinning back at her. "Why do they call you Buzz?"

"My parents claim that when I was a small child I was always talking, and if I didn't know the right word for what I wanted to say then I'd make a sort of high-pitched, buzzing sound. I still talk all the time even now."

She paused to study me. "I'm supposed to take you to another room. Are you able to walk the length of a corridor or two, or should I get a wheelchair?"

I tapped my dataview to fold it up, shoved it back into my pocket, and stood up. "I can walk."

"You're sure you won't faint or be sick?" Buzz wrinkled her nose and shuddered. "I've had one person throw up already today, and I don't want another one."

"I don't think I'll faint or be sick."

She nodded. "You can walk then, but warn me if you start feeling dizzy."

I followed Buzz out of the room and along the corridor. She waved her hand as we reached a drinks dispenser.

"Would you like something to drink, Amber?"

I was feeling thirsty, but I couldn't get Shanna's comment about the sewage reclamation system out of my head. "No, thank you."

Buzz turned into another corridor, opened a door labelled

"Therapy 6", and led me into a room that had the same battered white walls as the treatment room, but proper sleep field fittings instead of a bed, and a cushioned armchair. She gestured at the sleep field.

"You lie down, while I sit here and keep an eye on you. Tell me if you have any sick or dizzy spells, and I'll get the doctor to take another look at you."

I activated the sleep field, lay back on its cushion of warm air, and gave a sigh of relief.

Buzz sat down in the armchair. "You're obviously from Teen Level," she said chattily. "Are you one of the eighteen-year-olds about to go into Lottery?"

"No, I'm only seventeen, so Lottery is still a year away for me."

"I went through Lottery last year. I expected to be assigned to be a teacher like my parents, but ended up doing this job instead." She shrugged. "It just proves how hard it is to predict a Lottery result."

Teachers were all at least Level 40. I wondered what Buzz's parents thought of their daughter being assigned to run errands in the depths of the Hive. "Were you disappointed?"

"No, this is far better for me. I told you that I talk all the time – you must have noticed that yourself – and I love meeting new people. Now I have work where I get to talk to lots of different people." Buzz paused for breath. "What did you do to your head?"

"I bumped it on one of the stars in the ceiling of Teen Level beach."

Buzz burst out laughing. "You don't look tall enough to manage that."

I groaned. "I've a feeling I'll be hearing jokes like that for weeks. What happened was that I was doing the 'C' grade cliff climb with my eyes closed, missed the ledge at the top, and thumped my head on the ceiling."

She pulled a cross-eyed face at me. "Do you normally climb cliffs with your eyes closed?"

"I don't normally climb cliffs at all. I'm scared of heights.

Forge suggested that climbing the cliff might help my fear and… Well, I knew it was a bad idea, but I agreed to try it anyway. I find it hard to say no to him."

"Forge is a bully?"

"Oh no," I said hastily.

"Forge is a good looking boy then? You've got a crush on him?"

"I find it hard to say no to Forge, but I'm sure that isn't because I've got a crush on him. At least, I'm almost sure."

I hesitated. I'd never discussed this with anyone before today. I couldn't possibly talk about it to Shanna, because she was Forge's girlfriend, and confiding in anyone else in our corridor group could lead to trouble as well. I'd considered trying to explain it to my mother on one of my weekly visits home, but decided that she either wouldn't understand or would get worried. It was far easier to tell things to a stranger, especially one as friendly and talkative as Buzz.

"If I did have a crush on Forge," I continued, "then I'd surely want him to be my boyfriend, and I don't. Forge is in a relationship with my best friend, and I'm happy for both of them."

Buzz pursed her lips. "If it's a crush, then it's an unusual one. I had a crush on a stunningly good looking boy on Teen Level, and I was so desperate to get him to kiss me that I deliberately jammed the controls on a lift to get us stuck in there alone together."

I giggled. "Did it work?"

"Oh yes. It worked absolutely splendidly. We had a glorious fifteen minutes before Emergency Services rescued us." She gave me a wicked grin. "You wouldn't want to trap Forge in a lift with you?"

I shook my head.

"Is Forge a charismatic leader type?"

"Definitely."

"Then perhaps that's your explanation. The boy is naturally persuasive."

"I suppose it might be that," I said doubtfully.

"Has this situation been going on for long?"

I was too embarrassed to admit that it had been going on since the day I moved to Teen Level. "For a while."

"Has it caused you problems before?"

"Not really. Forge spends a lot of time surfing and swimming, so I got drawn into trying both of those. I gave up surfing after a nasty wipe out, but I enjoy swimming."

"Forge didn't try to pressure you into carrying on with the surfing?" asked Buzz.

"No. I'm sure he won't pressure me to try cliff climbing again either." I was regretting trying to explain the Forge issue, and tried to end the discussion. "It's never been a real problem. I just felt that my reaction to Forge was a bit strange."

"Have you tried dating any of the other boys on Teen Level?"

I was startled by the question. "Not yet. Do you think that dating someone else would stop me reacting oddly to Forge?"

"It might. Even if it didn't, a few dates would hopefully be fun for both you and the boy." Buzz gave me a thoughtful look. "You still aren't experiencing any sickness or dizziness?"

"I feel perfectly well."

"I'm not seeing any signs of memory loss or confusion." Buzz leaned back in her chair, briefly stared up at the ceiling, and then gave a decisive nod. "I don't see any need to keep you here overnight, Amber. I'll take you back to the reception desk and authorize your discharge now."

CHAPTER FOUR

I gave Buzz an incredulous look. "You'll authorize my discharge? Are you allowed to do that?"

"Yes. A doctor has already treated your injury and prescribed tablets for you to take back to Teen Level. You just needed a psychologist to check you for signs of certain possible complications."

"I didn't know you were a psychologist," I muttered, trying to remember exactly what I'd said to her.

She smiled. "Well, I am, and I'm happy to clear you for immediate discharge. Your head will probably continue hurting you for a few days. You can take one of your tablets every six hours to help with that. If you're still in pain a week from now, or you find yourself experiencing any memory issues or blurred vision, then you should contact me again. You'll be sent a copy of your medical discharge report. If you call the number on that, it will come straight through to me."

I was still struggling to adjust to this situation. "But you don't look high enough level to be a…" I realized how rude that must sound, and broke off my sentence.

"I'm a Level 1 Psychological Therapist."

Level 1! I gaped at her, stunned and appalled. I'd been chattering away to a Level 1 Psychological Therapist.

Buzz laughed. "There's no need to look so worried, Amber. I work with patients on many different levels of the Hive. There are several techniques for encouraging patients to relax and talk about their fears. When I'm working with low level patients, I find the simplest and most effective method is to wear low level clothing. Visual messages and body language can often be far more important than words. Instead of being an intimidating, well-dressed, superior member of the Hive, I make myself approachable, literally putting myself on the same level as my patients."

Buzz stood up, and I hastily rolled out of the sleep field and stood up myself. She gave me another of her infectious grins, before leading the way out of the room.

"The people who live in nearby apartments to me get very confused by my varying clothes. I met a new neighbour yesterday when I was wearing Level 80 clothing. He thought I was there to clean the corridors, and helpfully pointed out a smear on the wall."

I gave a bewildered laugh.

"I'm planning to call on him this evening, and watch the poor man's face when I explain who I really am," added Buzz. "He's deliciously handsome, so I think I'll wear the new dress that I bought last week. It manages to be frighteningly respectable while dreadfully suggestive at the same time."

Buzz babbled on about her new neighbour during the walk to the reception desk, and the processing of my discharge, then waved farewell. As I headed through the double doors, a packet of tablets in my hand, I could hear she was already chattering away to her next patient.

Once back in the open area outside, I paused to put the tablets in my pocket and look around. If I went along the corridor on my left, I knew I'd reach an express lift. The problem was that I'd been strapped on a stretcher in that lift, with a grey-masked nosy staring down at me and reading my thoughts. I knew it was an irrational reaction, but I never wanted to set foot in that particular lift again.

I could see apartment doors in the corridor straight ahead of me, so I turned to walk down the corridor to my right. There weren't any doors on this corridor, just wall murals with park scenes. Given the clue from the murals, I wasn't surprised to reach a junction, where there were double doors with the green park symbol on my left, and a corridor with a set of slow, medium and express belts on my right.

I stopped walking to think. I was on Level 93 of the Hive, somewhere almost vertically below Teen Level beach, so I'd be close to the boundary between Turquoise Zone and Green Zone. I had to get back up to Teen Level, and then take the belt system south to my room in Blue Zone.

I was feeling tired and strained. My head was starting to ache too. It was tempting to have a rest in a park before facing the journey, but I'd no right to trespass in a Level 93 park. I wasn't even sure what parks would be like on such a low level of the Hive.

There was a sudden squeal of excitement, and two small girls ran past me. They couldn't have been more than three years old, so they struggled to open the park doors. I stepped forward to help them, and automatically followed them inside.

I found myself standing on a gravel path, and shaded my eyes with my right hand while they adjusted to the glare of the park suns overhead. The two girls were heading to join a group of other children in a sand filled play area to my right. A green flash came from the right wrist of one of the girls, which meant an anxious parent was checking the location of her tracking bracelet.

I laughed, remembering how often my parents had checked my location when I was a child, how embarrassing I'd found it, and how relieved I'd been to reach the great age of ten years old and be free from my tracking bracelet. Becoming thirteen, and moving to Teen Level, had been a far less welcome milestone, and now the even more significant age of eighteen was growing ominously close.

I shook my head to banish that thought, and looked round at my surroundings. I saw a grove of dwarf oak trees to my left, and a large grassy area straight ahead of me, where an activity leader was showing a gaggle of children how to do a complex Carnival dance involving glittering silver ribbons. The older ones of about ten or eleven were making a good attempt at copying him, but there were a couple of five-year-old boys who were just running in circles round a nearby structural pillar, waving their streamers and screaming in excitement.

Everything about this park brought back reassuring memories of my childhood on Level 27. I'd played in a bigger sandpit, I'd danced on grass that was mowed more frequently, and the flower beds had had a richer range of colours, but this park was in a better state than the one I frequented now on Teen Level.

Three men were walking towards me, one of them gesticulating wildly as he explained something to the other two. I stepped aside to let them reach the exit door, and then followed the gravel path. It reached a stream, and I paused to peer into one of the pools. Yes, there were fish swimming there. Again, not such multi-coloured fish as I remembered from the Level 27 park, but no different to those on Teen Level.

I was feeling horribly thirsty now, so I walked on looking for a refreshment kiosk. Apartments might be smaller on Level 93 than on Level 27, but the parks seemed to be at least as large, if not even larger.

I finally saw a red and white striped kiosk standing near the edge of a small lake, and was hurrying towards it when a blue-clad hasty appeared from a side path. She turned to frown at me, and I froze guiltily.

"Have you had an accident?" she asked. "Do you need medical treatment?"

I peered down at my tunic, and saw the dark marks of bloodstains streaked across the blue lettering that proclaimed me a supporter of the Blue Zone teen surfing team. "I had an accident on Teen Level beach, and was taken for treatment at the medical facility down the corridor from here."

I knew the hasty would be asking for my identity code next to check my story. That would be followed by questions about why I was walking round this park instead of going straight back to Teen Level, so I hurried on to offer my defence. "I've got a long journey home, and I'm still feeling tired and shaken after my accident, so I thought I'd rest here in the park for a while before heading back."

I braced myself for the inevitable lecture about how I should have taken a lift straight back to Teen Level and rested in a park there, and was stunned when the woman just smiled.

"That's a good idea."

She walked over to a nearby bench and sat down. I looked after her, confused that her behaviour was so different to the hasties I'd met when I visited my parents. Then I realized the obvious point. My parents lived on Level 27, and I was on Level 93 now. Clearly the hasties were more worried about people trespassing on high levels of the Hive than low levels.

There was a shrill bleep from the direction of the hasty, and an automated voice spoke. "Hazard perimeter breach. Path 4. Rushton 2527-0355-317."

The hasty jumped to her feet, and hurried off to intercept a small boy who was ignoring the flashing red bracelet on his right wrist and heading for the lake. I laughed as I saw her shake her head at him, and sternly point the way back to the approved, child-safe area of the park. Now that was exactly like the behaviour of hasties on Level 27.

My headache was getting steadily worse now, so I decided I should take one of the tablets I'd been given. I'd definitely need a drink for that, so I moved on to the refreshment kiosk.

An elderly man stood at the counter. He stared at the bloodstains on my tunic, and asked the same question as the hasty. "Do you need medical help?"

"I've had medical treatment, thank you. I just want to buy a drink."

The man nodded. "If you're hungry as well, then our meal deal is the best value. That includes a free bottle of drink and a crunch cake."

I studied the poster with the kiosk price list, and was relieved to see things were barely more expensive than on Teen Level. I decided I was hungry as well as thirsty now, and the man was right about the meal deal being the best value.

"I'll have the cheese meal deal, with chocolate crunch cake, and do you have a melon flavoured drink?"

He laughed and pointed at my tunic. "You're not just far from your home zone, but far from your home level as well."

I gave him a confused look.

"If you were on Level 93 to visit your parents, then you'd know we only have the basic apple, orange or lemon drinks," he explained gently. "Asking for melon drinks shows you've lived far higher up the Hive."

I wasn't sure how to reply to the comment about levels, so I stuck to the topic of drinks. "In that case, I'll have an apple drink, please."

A minute later, I had a large bottle tucked under my right arm, and was holding a huge chunk of bread smothered with cheese and mixed salad in my right hand and a crunch cake in my left hand. A bevy of lake ducks were advancing on me optimistically, so I retreated to a quiet spot by the stream where I just had a single, hopeful rabbit watching me.

I took one of my tablets, gulped down some of my apple drink, and then started eating. I was halfway through my meal before I remembered Shanna's comment about Level 93 being close to the sewage reclamation systems on Level 100.

I hesitated for a second, and then told myself that Shanna's remark had been ridiculous. Our Hive city was underground, and all our water and air was recycled, but the reclaimed water and stale air went through full purification on Level 100 before being sent back into the supply systems. The water here on Level 93 couldn't be any different from the water higher up the Hive.

I started eating again. The bread was fresh, the cheese had a strong but pleasant taste, and the drink and the crunch cake couldn't be faulted. The salad leaves were too coarse and bitter for my taste, so I shared them with the rabbit before stretching out on the grass with a sigh of repletion.

The tablet was obviously working, because the pain in my head had eased. I lay in blissful idleness, admiring the violet flowers on a group of nearby bushes, and listening to the birdsong coming from the trees. Occasionally, a small bird would swoop above me, heading for a nest box attached to the top of a nearby structural pillar.

I wasn't sure if it was the effect of the tablet, or my large meal, but I found myself yawning heavily. I closed my eyes, intending to have a short doze before heading back to my room on Teen Level, but woke to find the sun-effect lights in the ceiling had dimmed to moon brightness, and the tiny lights of stars had appeared.

If the park lighting had switched to the night setting, then it had to be past ten o'clock in the evening. I'd slept for over six hours!

I sat up in alarm, and looked round to see the welcoming park of earlier had become a place of ominous dark shadows.

CHAPTER FIVE

Level 93 had seemed reassuringly like Teen Level earlier, but now I was conscious of being over forty levels and a zone away from my home corridor. I scrambled to my feet, groped my way round a dark mass of bushes, and headed back towards where the lights of moons were reflected in the smooth lake water. I'd never had any problems finding my way round our area park on Teen Level at night, but I wasn't familiar with the paths here, and I'd no idea where the exits were.

My best plan was to find the refreshment kiosk again. It would be closed for the night, but it would still be a useful guide to finding an exit, because a park kiosk was always on the major path through a park.

Finding the kiosk was harder than I expected. Its red and white stripes had been instantly noticeable in the daytime, but now it was just another shadowy shape among those of trees and structural pillars. Once I reached it, I had a choice of going left or right along the path. Both directions should lead to a park exit. I turned left and soon reached double doors that had a glowing green exit sign.

I hurried through the doors, feeling buoyant with relief, and saw I was at the edge of a brightly lit shopping area. Despite the late hour, there were a surprising number of people moving from shop to shop. I supposed there were a lot of shift workers living here on Level 93.

I headed across to a row of lifts, summoned one, and the

doors opened to show a man and woman wearing matching white overalls. I glanced at the destination level number, saw they were heading up to one of the fifty industrial levels right at the top of the Hive, and set the lift controls for Teen Level 50. There didn't seem to be many people travelling between levels so late in the evening, because the lift zoomed upwards without stopping for anyone else.

When the doors opened on Teen Level, I saw I was in another shopping area. Teens had little reason to shop late at night, so the lights were turned down, and only a handful of shadowy figures were in sight. I was still at the wrong side of Turquoise Zone, but I felt far more comfortable now I was back on my home level.

I walked towards a brighter area of lights, and saw it marked a major belt interchange. I checked the signs. I was at 505/5010 in Turquoise Zone, and I had to get home to 510/6120 in Blue Zone. I stepped onto the southbound slow belt, and gave myself a second to adjust to the speed before moving across to the medium, and then the express belts.

I was being carried along an extra wide corridor with bright lights overhead. There was a large chattering group of teens ahead of me, and a boy and girl standing behind me. The group ahead must have been to a late night party on Teen Level beach, because they were all carrying beach bags and towels. I realized I'd left my own bag and towel behind when I was taken away on the stretcher. Hopefully one of my friends would have had enough sense to take them back for me.

The signs on the wall showed that we were approaching the bulkhead between Turquoise Zone and Blue Zone. I was working out exactly how many minutes it would take me to get back to my room from there, when the smooth running express belt under me seemed to falter for a moment, and then started gradually slowing. I looked round in confusion, and saw the medium belt was slowing too.

Alarmed now, I turned to the boy and girl behind me. "What's happening? Is the belt system breaking down?"

The girl pulled a pitying face at my stupidity. "The three-monthly test closure of the Hive bulkhead doors starts at midnight. Did you really think the express belts would be left running at high speed during that, so they keep throwing people at closed bulkhead doors?"

"Oh, yes. A lot has been happening today, so I'd completely forgotten the bulkhead door test was tonight. Silly of me." I hastily turned to face forward again.

"Now there's someone who'll be coming out of Lottery as a Level 99 Sewage Technician," said the girl's contemptuous voice from behind me.

I cringed in embarrassment, but I had a bigger problem than looking a fool in front of a couple of strange teens. If I didn't make it through the bulkhead doors before they closed, then I'd be stuck in Turquoise Zone for an extra hour.

All three belts were running at slow belt speed now. Red signs started flashing, and a deafening voice came from overhead. "Warning, zone bulkhead approaching! Bulkhead doors are about to close. All passengers leave the belts now."

I shuffled my way across the medium and slow belts, and stepped on to the corridor floor. The group of teens ahead of me was walking forward, so I followed them on to where the corridor ended in an open area.

I could see the two massive blue and turquoise striped bulkhead doors now. They were wide open as usual, so I thought I still had a chance to get through before the test closure, but then I saw that blue-uniformed hasties were stretching red tape across them.

A man in a maintenance uniform stood in front of the bulkhead doors. He took out his dataview and spoke into it. "Bulkhead 6, Door 17, Level 50. We are clear to close on Turquoise side."

The watching teens were taking out their dataviews too and checking the time. There was an expectant pause and then they started chanting. "Five, four, three, two..."

The voices were drowned out by a siren screaming, and then the two great bulkhead doors started sliding together. The Hive was one zone wide and ten zones long. I pictured this scene being repeated at every door on each of the nine bulkheads, on all the hundred accommodation levels and fifty industrial levels of the Hive.

When I was eight years old, our teachers had taken us on a special midnight trip to watch the bulkhead doors close. They'd given us lectures on the importance of being able to shut off areas of the Hive in cases of severe emergency like a great fire. I'd barely listened to any of it. My mind had been focused on the Hive Duty songs we'd been taught in school, remembering all the lines about the Hive being one great community working together for the good of all, and shuddering at the idea of Blue Zone being sealed off from the rest of the Hive.

Now I was seventeen years old, but I still felt an echo of that old terror as I looked at the sealed bulkhead doors. I'd lived in Blue Zone all my life, first on Level 27 and then on Level 50, but now it was impossible to reach it.

The man in maintenance uniform was talking into his dataview again. "Bulkhead 6, Door 17, Level 50. Confirming bulkhead doors sealed."

I wasn't sure what to do now. The bulkhead doors would be closed for at least an hour. I was feeling tired, and my head hurt, so I couldn't stand here for that long, but I couldn't think where else to go.

I spotted several teens moving purposefully through the crowd, turned my head to see where they were going, and saw they were heading towards a set of chairs. I hurried after them, and sat down with a feeling of relief.

More teens joined us, and then a man came to stand in front of us. I saw his activity leader uniform and had a ghastly moment of realization. I'd gatecrashed a Turquoise Zone activity session!

"I'm glad that so many of my class made the effort to get here." The activity leader turned his head to look directly at me. "We seem to have a new recruit as well. Shouldn't you be at a Blue Zone lecture on bulkhead doors?"

I heard a giggle from the girl sitting next to me. "I had an accident," I said awkwardly. "I had to go to a medical facility for treatment, and I didn't make it through the bulkhead doors before they closed, so..."

"Ah, I see," the activity leader interrupted me. "You were delayed by your accident, couldn't get to your own class, so you decided to join our lecture instead."

"Yes," I said.

"What's your name?"

"Amber."

"I like your dedication, Amber." The man faced the class again. "Now if you were paying attention in yesterday's activity session, you'll know half the maintenance staff in our Hive will be taking part in this exercise."

He took out his dataview, tapped it, and displayed a complex diagram on the wall. "As you see, the bulkhead doors extend above ceiling height and below floor level. There are people in vents and conduits right now, checking that every way through for fire, smoke and toxic fumes is blocked."

I sat back in my chair, letting his voice drone on past me. He'd been talking for what seemed like hours, and I was on the edge of falling asleep, when I heard a different voice speak. I hastily forced my eyes open again, looked round, and tensed as I saw the activity leader had finished his lecture and was now asking people questions.

"The main vertical air vent," said the boy who was sitting two chairs away from me.

"Wrong." The activity leader looked at the girl next to me. "Magda?"

"The waste chute."

"Wrong." The activity leader looked at me. "Amber?"

I'd no idea what question I was supposed to be answering. I threw a desperate look at the diagram. There were lots of labels on it, so I picked one at random.

"The bypass electrical link."

The activity leader's head went back as if he was startled, and he jabbed a finger at me. "You are right!"

I was? I wondered what I was right about. At that moment, the siren sounded again, and everyone turned their heads to watch the bulkhead doors sliding open.

"My class, you've had a late night so I'll let you off tomorrow morning's activity session," said the activity leader briskly. "Amber, this is for you. Congratulations."

He held out his hand. I was stunned to see the gold card he was holding.

"Amber," he repeated.

I made myself stand up and go to accept the card. "Thank you," I muttered.

The other teens dutifully applauded the gold card presentation, but I could see the resentment in their faces as they did it, and they stood up and hurried off without speaking to me. The hasties had removed their red tape, so I joined the rush of people hurrying through to Blue Zone.

The belt system was already speeding up again. Within a couple of minutes, I was travelling south at full express speed. I looked down at the gold card in my hand and felt like crying. I'd spent four years working hard, going to all the activity sessions, and I'd only been given a gold card once for my swimming. Now I'd dozed through a lecture, made a lucky guess at answering a question, and been handed a gold card that entitled me to attend advanced sessions in engineering.

I thrust the gold card into my pocket, and tried to forget about it for the rest of my journey. Once I reached 505/6120, I just had a short ride on an eastbound belt, and I was at the end of my home corridor. I gave a sigh of relief, walked down to my room, opened the door, and froze in shock.

There was a gaping hole in my room wall, and a black-clad creature with weird glowing eyes was climbing, spider-like, out of it.

CHAPTER SIX

I made a faint squeaking sound and took a step backwards. What sort of monster could have glowing eyes like this? I remembered the telepath that had been in the lift with me, and how there'd been a strange glint of purple eyes behind her grey mask. Was this what a telepath looked like without their mask? If it was, then why was a telepath coming through the wall of my room?

"Don't worry, Amber," said a familiar voice. "It's only me."

"Forge?" I shrieked.

"Please don't shout like that. You'll wake everyone up."

I forced my voice down to a savage whisper. "You scared me to death. What are you doing in my room?"

"There's absolutely no need to get upset."

"No need to get upset?" I repeated incredulously. "You've destroyed the wall of my room!"

"No, I haven't. How is your head feeling?"

"My head was feeling fine until you leapt out of the wall at me."

I'd left the lights in my room on minimum setting. Now I finally had the sense to turn them up to full brightness. Forge stood in front of the hole in the wall, looking guilty and embarrassed. He was wearing a black top and leggings, his face and hands were grubby, and he had a coil of rope slung over his shoulder. What I'd thought were weird glowing eyes, were actually lights attached to a black band tied round his forehead.

Forge lifted both his hands in a pacifying gesture, and spoke in soothing tones. "I'd never have come in here if I'd known you were coming back tonight, Amber. I promise that I haven't damaged anything. I just took off the cover of the air vent inspection hatch on your wall so I could look inside. I was careful not to make a mess."

He paused to look down at the heap of clothes on the floor. "That mess was already here when I arrived."

I wasn't going to get diverted onto the subject of my untidiness. "How did you get in here?"

"You told me your door code."

"I did? When?"

"Last year," said Forge. "We were supposed to meet for swimming training. You called me to say you'd be late back from visiting your parents, and wanted to go straight to the swimming pool. You asked me to pick up your swimming bag and meet you there."

He was right. "You still remember my door code after all this time?"

"It's not hard to remember a door code that's 54321."

I wasn't going to get diverted onto the subject of my choice of door codes either. "Why can't you mess around with the inspection hatch in your own room?"

"There isn't an inspection hatch in my room. I thought you wouldn't mind me opening this one and taking a peek inside."

I glared at him. "Those are your cliff climbing clothes. You dressed in your cliff climbing outfit, tied those silly lights to your head, and brought along a rope just to peek inside an inspection hatch?"

"Well, not exactly," admitted Forge. "When I looked inside the hatch, and saw the vent was big enough to wriggle through, I couldn't resist climbing in there to take a look, but my ordinary clothes kept getting snagged on the mesh floor and it was pitch dark. I did the sensible thing, went back to my own room, and got better equipped before exploring further."

I groaned. "That's your idea of being sensible? Going crawling round a filthy vent system?"

Forge looked down at his hands, and rubbed them on his top. "It wasn't that dirty."

"You'd no way of knowing what was in there. You could have fallen down a lift shaft!"

"That's why I brought the rope," said Forge, "but I found that I didn't need it. The narrow vent led into a bigger maintenance crawl way, with motion-triggered lighting. That joined other crawl ways, and there were points with ladders leading up and down."

He shook his head. "It was a really confusing place. There were maintenance codes on the walls in places, but I didn't understand what they meant. Next time I go in there, I plan to take a marker pen to number the junctions and ladders so…"

"You aren't going back in there," I interrupted him. "At least, you aren't going back in there from *my* room. Fix that hole in my wall right away!"

Forge sighed, went back to the hole in the wall, lifted a cover over it, and locked it into place. He stepped back and pointed at it. "You see. There's no damage done at all."

I inspected the cover, and prodded it with a dubious finger to see if it would fall off the wall. It didn't.

"I'm really keen to go back in there a few more times and explore," added Forge hopefully, "and yours is the only room on our corridor with a full size inspection hatch. Everyone else just has tiny little air vents."

"Everyone else is lucky," I said bitterly. "How can I sleep knowing that people could crawl out of my wall at any moment?"

"Please, Amber."

Forge gave me a pleading look. I felt the usual compulsion to agree to what he wanted, but fought against it. "No. You're never setting foot in my room again."

"But it was so exciting exploring the maintenance crawl ways."

"You go cliff climbing. You're in the Blue Zone teen swimming and surfing teams. That's more than enough excitement for any reasonable person." I pointed at the door. "Go!"

Forge sighed again and left. I looked gloomily at the closed door, wondered if any of our friends had seen him coming out of my room in the middle of the night, and if they'd suspect something was going on between us. It seemed highly unlikely. If Shanna was a park light set to sun brightness, then I was barely the equivalent of a light at moon setting.

I turned to look at my reflection in the wall mirror. My hair was a wild disaster and my tunic was smeared with dark bloodstains. I pulled a face at myself. Forget a park light at moon setting; I was merely one of the tiny, faint stars.

I hung one of my big swimming towels over the inspection hatch on the wall, to make sure no one crawling through the vent system could peek through its grille at me, and then stripped off my clothes. I dumped them with the heap already on the floor, made a mental note that I really must do some laundry soon, and went into my shower cubicle to have a brief and cautious wash.

The glue on my scalp seemed to survive the hot water without problems, but my head was aching again. It was well over six hours since I'd taken my last tablet, so I could take another one now. I remembered the tablet box was still in my tunic pocket, and retrieved it from the laundry heap. As I took out one of the tablets, I noticed the warning words on the box. "May cause drowsiness."

I groaned. That explained why I'd fallen asleep in the Level 93 park. If I'd noticed those words earlier, I'd never have taken a tablet while I was there, I'd have got back to rejoin my friends in the early evening, and Forge wouldn't have invaded my room and given me a phobia of inspection hatches.

I looked dubiously at the tablet I was holding, decided that causing drowsiness didn't matter when I was going to bed anyway, and swallowed it. I set the room lights to minimum, turned on the sleep field, relaxed on the warm cushion of air, and then frowned. I always slept with my head at the end of the sleep field closest to the wall with the air vent, but now I had a towel hanging next to my head.

I rolled out of the sleep field, and climbed on again the other way round, so the towel was by my feet. It made occasional billowing movements as air blew from the vent, but I forced myself to ignore it and closed my eyes.

Perversely, the second tablet didn't seem to be having the

same effect as the first. I hovered on the edge of sleep, but couldn't cross the boundary. Disjointed memories of the day's events drifted through my mind. Atticus calmly breaking Teen Level conventions by telling me that his parents were Level 80. The ghastly moment in the lift when the telepath looked down at me. How I'd told Buzz about my odd reaction to Forge.

I'd assumed Buzz was just a chatty, low level stranger, keeping an eye on me in case I suffered dizziness from my head injury. If I'd known she was a Level 1 Psychological Therapist, would I have kept quiet about the whole Forge thing, or would I have given her more details, even mentioned a weird recurring dream I had about him?

At least I'd made a breakthrough tonight. Forge had wanted to explore the air vents again, but I'd been so angry about him invading the privacy of my room that I'd refused.

I was savouring that small victory, and thinking I'd have to change the door code of my room tomorrow, when I finally fell asleep. I dreamed I was in the park on Level 93 again. I was feeding salad leaves to the rabbit, and it was talking to me, telling me that Lottery had assigned it to be a Level 1 Psychological Therapist.

Then somehow the rabbit turned into Forge, and I was caught in that strange recurring dream. Forge and I were walking through a park. Forge was taller than usual, the trees were taller than usual too, and the suns in the ceiling were blindingly bright.

A ringing noise invaded my dreams, and I was dragged into consciousness. I had a moment of disorientation before I worked out that it must be eight o'clock in the morning, and my dataview was ringing to tell me it was time to wake up.

I reached out for where my dataview lay on the table next to my sleep field, banged my knuckles painfully hard on the wall, and remembered I'd been sleeping the wrong way round. I wriggled to face the opposite direction in the sleep field, grabbed my dataview, and then realized the ringing sound was actually coming from my room door chime.

I rolled out of the sleep field, and tugged on a robe before shouting through the door. "Who is it?"

"It's me," said Forge.

I opened the door and glared at him. "What's the matter with you, Forge? First you scare me to death in the middle of the night, and now you wake me up early."

"It's not early," said Forge. "When I got up this morning, I told the others you'd got back late last night. When you didn't appear for our Carnival mask painting session, we thought you were sleeping late, but once it got to eleven o'clock we started getting worried. Shanna was still busy painting the masks, so I said I'd check on you."

"It can't be eleven o'clock." I'd thrust my dataview into my pocket. I took it out again and glanced at it. "Oh, you're right, it is eleven o'clock. Waste it. Tell the others that I'm sorry for not helping with the masks. The doctor gave me some tablets that made me sleep for hours."

"It doesn't matter about the masks. We all understand you need rest after hurting your head. We were just worried in case you were ill." Forge paused to give me a wistful smile. "Is there any chance of you letting me go through your room to get into the vent system again? I'd be really grateful."

I opened my mouth, intending to say no. "Yes, but you must always ask my permission in future."

"I promise," Forge said joyfully, and hurried off down the corridor.

I stared after him. I'd been furious about Forge terrifying me last night. I'd been determined to never let him enter my room again. I'd intended to change my room door code to make sure he couldn't sneak in there without my knowledge. Now I'd just agreed to let him traipse through my room whenever he wanted.

I'd no idea what was wrong with me, why I kept acting this way with Forge when I could happily say no to anyone else and stick to it, but this had to stop right now.

CHAPTER SEVEN

I showered, dressed, and frowned at the tiny kitchen unit in the corner of my room. I was ravenously hungry, but the kitchen units in Teen Level rooms only delivered the most basic range of reconstituted meals. You could get much better food elsewhere for the same price, so I only resorted to using my kitchen unit when I was especially desperate.

I decided I'd wait to eat, arranged my hair to cover the glue, and headed for our corridor community room. I entered to find that everyone in our corridor group, with the notable exception of Reece, was inspecting an array of Carnival masks on the tables.

"I'm sorry I overslept," I said.

Everyone turned to face me, and Shanna gasped in horror. "Amber, what happened to your hair?"

"The doctor put some glue stuff on my scalp. Don't worry. The doctor said the glue will vanish naturally in about ten days' time."

"Ten days," repeated Shanna, in apocalyptic tones. "You mean you'll be looking like that all through Carnival?"

"Yes."

She gave a despairing sigh. "Given you had your medical treatment on Level 93, I suppose we should be grateful that you still have hair at all."

I hastily changed the subject. "I see you've finished painting the masks."

"I helped with the undercoat," said a paint-splattered Casper.

"You did a great job with the undercoat," said Linnette.

"We mustn't touch the masks because they aren't dry yet," added Casper.

"I'll be careful not to touch them." I moved to inspect the masks. Carnival masks were usually silver and gold, but these had tiny hints of blue as well, that added an extra touch of delicate distinction. "These are incredible."

"Shanna did all the clever finishing touches," said Preeja.

Shanna came to stand next to me, and looked proudly down at her work. "My parents told me that all the elite levels of the Hive are using blue as the accent colour for this Carnival."

Shanna had never said it explicitly, but the occasional comment like this had made it clear that her parents were either dress or decor designers for the highest levels of the Hive. I thought that Lottery would allocate Shanna similar work as well. I wished that I had even a tenth of her talent.

"I see Reece isn't here," I said.

"I told him he was excluded yesterday evening," said Forge grimly. "He pushed his way in here this morning anyway, and started upsetting Casper, so I threw him out. I don't know where Reece went after that."

"He's probably found someone else to annoy." I dismissed Reece with a wave of my hand. "It's my parents' day off work today, and I'm due to visit them this afternoon. I might as well set off now. I'm sure they won't mind me arriving an hour early."

"I'm sure they *expect* you to arrive an hour early," said Margot drily. "You go there an hour early every week, so you can get a free lunch."

I blushed. "Teen Level rules say we should limit ourselves to one afternoon or evening visit a week to our parents, and that visit shouldn't normally include a meal, but occasional exceptions are allowed."

Linnette laughed. "We all do the same thing. If we aren't begging free meals, we're taking dirty clothes home to save on the laundry machine charges. It's the only way to survive on a teen allowance."

She paused. "More importantly, Amber, are you well enough to visit your parents at all? You could call them and explain that you've had an accident and need to rest."

"No, I can't. They'd be dreadfully worried if I did that. Anyway, I'm feeling perfectly well now and extremely hungry."

I went out into the corridor. I wasn't surprised when Forge chased after me, glanced round warily, and spoke in urgent low tones.

"Amber, if you're going to visit your parents now, would this be a good time for me to...?"

I sighed. "I still don't understand the attraction of crawling round air vents, but I suppose so. Just make sure that you're out of there before I get back."

"I promise. Thank you." Forge dashed off to get ready for his thrilling expedition.

As a thirteen-year-old, I'd found it harrowing to leave my parents' apartment and live alone on Teen Level, but the Hive made sure that teens were still close to the support of their families. My room was in area 510/6120 on Teen Level 50, while my parents' apartment was in area 510/6120 on Level 27, just a lift ride away. It was only a few minutes before I was pressing the chime button next to their door.

When my mother opened the door, she hugged me, beckoned me inside, and started the ritual pretence that we went through every week. "You're a little early, so we haven't started our lunch yet. If you're hungry, then you can eat with us."

"That would be wonderful," I said. "I missed breakfast, so I'm starving."

I followed her through to the main living area. My father smiled at me, and my younger brother, Gregas, grunted something. Gregas had been quite sociable up until his twelfth birthday, but now he'd taken to communicating in a variety of grunts.

"Amber is hungry, so she'll be eating with us today," announced my mother, as if this was a highly unusual event instead of a regular bending of the Teen Level rules.

"By a fortunate coincidence, we've already set four places at the table," my father said, in mock solemnity.

Gregas made a higher pitched grunting sound this time. I thought it was intended to indicate amusement, but I wasn't fluent in grunts. It could just have meant that he was hungry and wanted to eat.

We moved to the table. There was the usual jug of melon juice. I eagerly poured out a glass full, gulped it down, and then refilled the glass again. I adored melon juice. I'd missed it terribly when I moved to Teen Level, so I always made the most of it on my visits home.

I briefly wondered how high a level I'd need to be after Lottery to be able to drink melon juice every day, but was distracted by my mother bringing a steaming bowl to the table.

"My favourite casserole," I said happily, and piled a large helping on my plate.

"Another fortunate coincidence," said my father, struggling to keep a straight face. "Please help yourself to a bread roll or three, Amber."

Gregas gave a sarcastic grunt.

"You shouldn't complain about these things, Gregas," said my father. "Remember that you'll be moving to Teen Level next year, and may be grateful for a few coincidences yourself."

For the next couple of minutes, I was too busy eating at high speed to spare time to speak, but then I slowed down a little. "I expect you've noticed my hair looks as if it needs combing. That's because I cut my head yesterday and the doctor treated it with special glue."

My mother frowned. "How did you cut your head? Were you badly hurt?"

I didn't want to explain that I'd hit my head on a star. My family were well aware that I was scared of heights, so there'd be questions about what I was doing up a cliff. "I bumped my head on something sharp. It wasn't serious, and the medical facilities on Teen Level were all very busy, so I was sent for treatment on Level 93."

"Level 93!" There was a group chorus. Even Gregas was shocked enough to join in with actual words rather than a grunt.

"Why did they send you to Level 93?" asked my father.

I shrugged, and quoted the title of one of the Hive Duty songs. "The Hive knows best."

"The Hive knows best," said my mother, "but... Level 93!"

I stared down at my plate, prodding chunks of casserole with my fork. The events of yesterday, and my worries about Lottery, were still churning round in my mind. Level 93 hadn't been so bad, I could adapt to living there, but my family's reaction to the mere mention of it had awakened my deepest fear.

I knew only too well that some parents would disown a child who came out of Lottery at an embarrassingly low level. It had happened to Margot's sister. I didn't know exactly what level Margot's parents were, but her sister had come out of last year's Lottery twenty levels lower than them.

Margot had been distraught when her parents cut off contact with her sister. Preeja and I had done what we could to help, ferrying sandwiches and drinks to Margot, and hiding the situation from everyone else by claiming Margot was staying in her room because she was ill.

There was no way to halt the unfolding disaster though. Margot had called her parents a dozen times, trying to convince them to change their minds, but they'd just ordered her to cut off contact with her sister as well. Margot defied them, was disowned in turn, and turned into a harder, bitter version of the girl she used to be.

Now I couldn't help picturing myself in the same position as Margot's sister. My parents were Level 27. Lottery could easily make me not just twenty, but fifty levels lower than them.

Somehow my emotions burst out into words. "Next year, I'll be entering Lottery. There's no way to predict your results, and I may end up rated Level 93 or even worse."

My mother gave me a startled look. "I'm sure you'll do brilliantly in Lottery, Amber."

"That's possible," I said, "but it's also possible that I'll do very badly. You need to think about that, and decide what level I need to be for you to keep..."

I broke off, appalled by my own words. Why had I said that?

Challenging my parents, demanding what level I'd need to be for them to keep treating me as their daughter, could only make a potential future disaster into something that would happen right now.

I remembered Margot's angry words from last year. "Once you know that your parents will casually dump you if Lottery rates you below a certain level, it shatters your whole relationship with them."

CHAPTER EIGHT

My father put his fork down and reached to pat my arm. "I'm sure you'll do well in Lottery, Amber, but even if you end up as Level 99, we promise that we will still be here for you."

"Of course we will," said my mother.

"We'll even promise to keep feeding you melon juice once a week," added my father.

The attempt at humour convinced me they really meant it. Relief swept over me and left me hovering on the edge of tears. I mustn't start crying. Gregas was already looking horrified at being dragged into such an emotional moment.

I desperately tried to get the conversation away from Lottery. "It was rather traumatic going to Level 93 yesterday. I was strapped on a stretcher, and a paramedic was taking me down in a lift, when a telepath squad joined us."

My mother gasped. "No wonder you're stressed and suffering from ridiculous worries. It must have been terrible for you, being trapped in a lift with one of those… repugnant creatures."

Gregas abruptly discovered words. "You can tell from their masks that nosies have peculiarly shaped heads. If you were in the lift with a nosy, you must have been very close to the creepy thing. Did you get a look under its mask?"

"Yes, I was very close to the nosy." I shuddered. "It was leaning over my stretcher, looking down at me, but I didn't see its face, only a glint of purple eyes."

Gregas looked horrified and thrilled at the same time. "My

friend, Wesley, says he saw a nosy take his mask off once, and there was a purple head underneath, with no hair or proper face at all, just saucer-shaped eyes."

"Stop upsetting your sister, Gregas," said my mother. "It's appalling that a telepath squad should force themselves on someone that's injured and helpless for no good reason. I'll complain to Health and Safety about it."

"Actually, the telepath squad did have a good reason for coming in my lift," I said. "They came to arrest the paramedic."

"You saw someone get arrested?" Gregas's eyes widened. "High up, Amber! What was the paramedic thinking about that got him arrested?"

I had a feeling that Gregas would soon be telling Wesley a lurid version of this story. "It sounded like the man was planning to hurt two people."

"He was? What will happen to him?" demanded Gregas.

"I don't know. The telepath mentioned corrective treatment."

Gregas gave a theatrical shudder. "Wesley says that his uncle worked with someone who got taken away by a telepath squad and they never saw her again."

"Wesley has an extremely overactive imagination," said my father. "Don't you remember when his parents moved to this corridor four years ago, and he told you they weren't his real parents? They'd just adopted him after he was traded here from another Hive."

"I should never have believed Wesley about that," admitted Gregas.

"No, you shouldn't," said my father. "While it's true that Hives trade a few people after Lottery to fill key vacancies, it's hard to imagine that our Hive had a desperate need for an eight-year-old boy with an addiction to coconut flavoured crunch cakes. I suspect that Wesley's statements about nosies are equally unreliable."

I suddenly had a new fear to add to my concerns about Lottery. What would it be like to come out of Lottery and be traded to another Hive? There were one hundred and six other Hive cities in the world. I'd heard a few of their names on our Hive news, and

I'd picked up the fact that some of them were smaller than our Hive and some were bigger, but I knew nothing about what life was like for their people.

We hadn't been taught anything about other Hives in school, because an ordinary loyal citizen of our Hive should have no interest in them, and anyone assigned to a profession in something like Hive Trade would be imprinted with all the information they needed. I'd heard whispered rumours of how conditions in other Hives were better or worse than our own, but they were probably just the wild imaginings of people like Wesley.

Was it possible that I'd come out of Lottery and discover the truth about other Hives by being traded to one of them? If that happened, then I'd never have any contact with my family again.

For a second, I was numbly picturing that horror, but then commonsense prevailed. People were only traded to fill positions that were utterly vital to the functioning of a Hive. For once, my total lack of talent for anything was reassuring. I definitely wouldn't be traded to an alien Hive, because none of them would want me.

"Don't you think so, Amber?" asked my father.

"What? Sorry, I was thinking of something and got distracted."

"I was saying that I find the presence of telepaths deeply unpleasant, but cases like your paramedic prove that they perform a vital service for the Hive. If your paramedic was thinking of harming people, then he had to be stopped before his thoughts became actions."

"I agree," I said.

"Let's forget about telepaths now, and enjoy the rest of our meal," said my mother. "Gregas mustn't be late for school."

Gregas groaned. "School is such a waste of time. I'm twelve years old. I can read, know my tables, can recite all the Hive Obligations, and sing all the Duty songs. Why do I have to keep spending three hours a day, five days a week in school when there's nothing left for me to learn? I'll be imprinted with all the other knowledge I need when I come out of Lottery."

It seemed as if every conversation I'd had in the last day or two kept coming back to the subject of Lottery. Were people mentioning it more because the Lottery of 2531 would be starting soon, or was it just that I was far more sensitive to every passing reference? I tried to force away thoughts of what it would be like to be imprinted, and ate the last few forkfuls of my casserole.

"After Carnival, your school lessons will concentrate on preparing you to move to Teen Level, Gregas," said my father. "You'll have plenty of new things to learn. Such as how to use laundry machines instead of dumping dirty clothes in a basket to reappear, magically folded and clean, on your shelves."

"How to budget so you can live comfortably on your teen allowance," said my mother.

"The limited range of food and drink on Teen Level," I said gloomily.

Gregas reverted to grunting an inaudible reply.

We had chocolate crunch cakes with cream drizzle for dessert, and then Gregas left for school. My parents and I watched one of the Hive entertainment channels after that, our attention divided between a thriller about a Hive England Defence team chasing a spy from another Hive, and a conversation about my parents' work developing new types of fruit and vegetables for the Hive hydroponics areas. There was, mercifully, no mention at all of Lottery.

When I finally left, I had a couple of illegal crunch cakes in my pocket. Rather than tamely going back to Teen Level in a lift, I headed for the shopping area, and walked across to the moving stairs in the centre. I gave one furtive look round for hasties, couldn't see any, and jumped on the handrail of the downway.

I balanced there precariously, as the moving handrail carried me down through the shopping areas on Level 28, Level 29, and Level 30. Strictly speaking, riding the rail was against the Hive safety rules, but it was accepted as a harmless teen gesture of rebellion, so I risked nothing more than a mild scolding from any hasty that spotted me.

I'd reached Level 33 when I heard the traditional warning whistle all the teens used, one low note, one high, one low, that meant hasties were about. I looked round to see who was whistling the warning, and saw a young man going past me on the upway. He looked as if he'd been through Lottery at least two or three years earlier, but he grinned at me, and made the T sign with his forefingers that signalled serious trouble.

I was puzzled, but waved my thanks at him, and jumped down to stand sedately on the moving stairs of the downway. When I reached the shopping area on Level 34, I saw why the man had been warning me. A group of a dozen hasties were standing near the moving stairs, studying everyone who went by, as if they were looking for someone in particular. I'd no idea what was going on, but judging from their grim expressions this wasn't a good time to be caught riding the handrail.

When I reached Teen Level 50, I walked along the corridors back to my room. When I opened the door, I half expected to find a hole in the wall, but the air vent inspection hatch cover was in place. The towel hanging over it had obviously been moved and then hung up again. I went across and adjusted it to cover the grille properly.

I grudgingly gave Forge credit for keeping his promise to be out of the vent system by the time I returned. I inspected the room suspiciously, but the only sign of disturbance was that the heap of dirty clothes on the floor had been shoved further into the corner.

There was a ringing sound from my door chime. I opened the door, expecting to see either Forge or Shanna, but it was Atticus. He held out a familiar bag and towel.

"I brought these back from the beach for you."

"Oh, thank you." I took them off him. "I'll need them for swimming training."

He stared down at his hands for a moment before speaking. "What I said to you about my parents being Level 80..."

"Don't worry. That was a private conversation so I won't tell anyone."

"That's not what I meant." He stared down at his hands again, then looked up at me and spoke in a rush. "I'd like you to be my partner for Carnival, Amber. I told you my parents were

Level 80 because I didn't want to mislead you into thinking I had a high level family like you."

I was stunned into silence. A boy from another corridor group had asked me to partner him last year, but I'd turned him down. Given the oddness of my reaction to Forge, I'd felt it best to stick to the Carnival parties for the younger teens and single people, where everyone danced the solo or communal ribbon dances.

Partnering someone for Carnival was a significant commitment. It meant spending three days of parties in their company, with the implication that the relationship would continue after that.

I dealt with the minor side issue first. "How did you know that my family was high level? I only had the set of basic possessions authorized under the Teen Level equality rules, and I never mentioned my parents' level to anyone."

He laughed. "When I arrived on Teen Level, it was clear who'd come from a high level of the Hive. You were shocked by how basic the rooms were, and mentioned food and drinks that we'd never had on Level 80."

I remembered my conversation with the man at the refreshment kiosk in the Level 93 park. "Things like melon juice?" I asked guiltily.

He nodded. "It only took me a minute looking up luxury items on my dataview to work out your parents' levels. Shanna's parents were elite. You were next highest of the girls, with parents who were at least Level 30. Forge was the highest of the boys, with parents who were at least Level 20."

"You've forgotten about Reece," I said. "His parents are elite."

Atticus laughed. "Reece keeps *claiming* his parents are elite, but that isn't true."

I blinked. "Reece has been lying about that?"

"Yes. Reece misunderstood something Shanna mentioned on the first day. He thought she was talking about a fruit when it was a type of cake, and she gave him a withering look. His parents are Level 40 at most."

Atticus looked at me expectantly. He was waiting for me to make a decision about being his partner for Carnival. Buzz had suggested it might be helpful to date someone, and that did make sense. Forge was my best friend's boyfriend, and we went swimming training together. I spent far more time with him than any other boy, so naturally I'd be focused on him.

I tried to force thoughts of Forge out of my mind. The important thing wasn't how I felt about Forge, but how I felt about Atticus. I certainly liked his quiet, serious nature, and I thought he was very intelligent. He fought a losing battle to keep his rebellious brown hair tidy, and he didn't have Forge's spectacular good looks or muscled build, but I found him attractive.

If I accepted Atticus as my partner for Carnival, then we'd be going to the parties for older teens in relationships, and things like kisses would be expected. The idea of kissing Forge made me feel deeply uncomfortable, but I could imagine enjoying kissing Atticus.

"You obviously hadn't realized I was building up to asking you to be my Carnival partner," said Atticus. "You'd better take some time to think about it and give me your answer tomorrow."

"I don't need time to think about it. I'd love to be your partner for Carnival."

"You're sure you don't mind about the level difference?"

"There's a level difference between our parents, but not between us. All teens are Level 50 and equal."

"That's wonderful." Atticus gave me a joyful smile. "Perhaps we could do some things together over the next few days, so we get comfortable with each other's company before the Carnival parties start."

"Yes, that would be a good idea. We're supposed to be at our community centre tomorrow morning for the next activity session on embroidery." I pulled a face. "Not that there's much point in me going. I was dreadful at the embroidery session last week. For that matter, I'm dreadful at most things. I've been to every type of activity session our community centre has offered since I came to Teen Level, and shown no sign of talent at any of them."

"You're good at swimming," said Atticus.

"Not good enough to be a professional swimmer."

"You're still doing better than me," said Atticus. "I seem to have no talents at all."

I shrugged. "Anyway, I'll be free tomorrow afternoon and evening."

"We could go to one of the evening parties on Teen Level beach."

"My doctor said I should stay away from Teen Level beach until the cut on my head heals, because wet sand might cause problems."

"We could just go to the park," said Atticus.

I frowned. "Linnette and Casper are park volunteers, and they'll be helping out there tomorrow afternoon."

"Does that matter? We aren't hiding this from our friends, are we?"

"No, we aren't. I only meant that we'd end up in a group with Linnette and Casper, and the idea was that we'd spend time alone together."

"That's true." Atticus paused to think. "The Blue Zone Arena has started running Light and Dark pageants in preparation for Carnival. We could go to the one tomorrow afternoon."

I didn't really enjoy Light and Dark pageants, but I'd already turned down two suggestions from Atticus so I felt I had to accept this one. "Yes, we can do that."

"Were you planning to eat lunch at the community centre after the activity session?"

I nodded. I got most of my meals at the community centre because it was the cheapest place to eat.

"I was planning to skip tomorrow morning's activity session," said Atticus, "but I think I'll go along after all. That way we can have lunch together before we go to the pageant."

There was an awkward moment. Were you supposed to kiss someone after agreeing to be their Carnival date? I wasn't sure, and Atticus didn't seem sure what to do either, but then I saw someone further down the corridor.

"Reece is watching us," I whispered a warning.

"I'd better go then. I'll see you later, Amber."

Atticus hurried off down the corridor, and I dodged back inside my room and shut the door to avoid Reece. I went across to the wall mirror and looked at my reflection. The lump of glue in my hair made it look like my head was as peculiarly shaped as a telepath's, but Atticus had still asked me to be his partner for Carnival. I'd definitely done the right thing accepting him. By the time Carnival was over, I'd probably have forgotten all about my odd reaction to Forge.

I was smiling foolishly at my reflection when a disembodied voice spoke from the end wall.

"Amber, it's me."

CHAPTER NINE

I turned round, marched across to the end wall of my room, and yanked the towel off the inspection hatch. "How dare you spy on me and Atticus!"

I couldn't see Forge's face through the grille, there was just a faint shadowy shape, but his voice sounded contrite. "I'm really sorry. I didn't do it deliberately. I got back here and found you'd put the inspection hatch cover back in place. I was about to ask you to let me out when I heard you talking to Atticus. I thought I should keep quiet until after he'd gone."

"It would have been better if you'd left for a while, instead of skulking in there and listening to us... Wait a minute." My brain finally processed Forge's comment about the hatch cover. "When I got back here, the cover was already in place, and the towel was hanging over it. I assumed you'd finished exploring the vents and put the cover back on before leaving."

"I didn't put the cover back on. If it wasn't you either, then who...?" Forge broke off his sentence and groaned. "It must have been Reece. He's been lurking round the corridor ever since we excluded him, trying to force his company on us. He must have seen me coming into your room, and followed me in here to see what I was doing."

"You should have locked the door behind you."

"I did lock the door."

"Then how did Reece get in?"

"It's not hard to work out a door code that's 54321," said

Forge. "When Reece found the inspection hatch cover off, he'd guess I was inside exploring the vent system. I suppose he thought it would be funny to put the cover back on so I couldn't get out."

I frowned. "I think you're right about it being Reece. He was watching me talk to Atticus."

"I'm sure I'm right," said Forge. "Can you let me out now please? You just need to turn the two catches on each side of the cover to release it. I think maintenance workers have a tool that lets them turn the catches from inside the vent system, but of course I don't have one of those."

I turned the catches. "The cover still seems to be locked in place."

"Have you turned all four catches?"

"Yes."

"That's odd. The cover must be stuck on. I'll give it a shove from my side. Be ready to catch it when it comes loose."

"I'm ready." I waited expectantly, but nothing happened.

"It's still stuck," said Forge. "Stand well back and I'll kick it free."

I retreated to the far end of the room. There were a series of loud clangs. The inspection hatch cover still didn't move.

"Can you check if Reece used something to wedge the cover in place?" asked Forge's breathless voice.

I went back to study the cover. It was bulging in the middle from Forge's kicks. I couldn't see anything wedging it in place, but there was a glistening look to the edges.

"Have you found anything?" asked Forge.

I prodded the edge of the cover with a wary finger, and then leaned forward to sniff at it. There was a faint odour that I remembered from a recent activity session at the community centre.

"Bad news," I said. "Reece has glued the inspection hatch cover in place, and I think he's used the permanent bond glue."

"You mean the stuff where you need the right solvent to remove it?" asked Forge.

"I'm afraid so, and we'd need an awful lot of solvent to get that cover loose. We'll have to call Emergency Services to get you out."

"We can't do that," said Forge. "Do you remember the climbing instructor said that she was going to report Reece's behaviour to Health and Safety?"

"Vaguely."

"Well, a telepath squad turned up to see Reece yesterday evening, so the rest of us went off to hide in the community centre. When we got back, Reece started screaming insults at me."

"Why?"

Forge shrugged. "He assumed I was the one who'd told the climbing instructor his identity code. Once he finished yelling abuse at me, he started calling you names as well, saying it was all your fault for getting stuck on the cliff."

"You didn't tell Reece that it was Margot who gave away his identity code?"

"No. I didn't want him targeting Margot instead of me. I just said that we'd voted to exclude him from our corridor group until after Carnival, and walked away. I think Reece has trapped me in here to get his revenge on both of us. If we call Emergency Services to get me out, then I'll be in trouble for exploring the air vents, and you'll be in trouble for helping me get in there."

"Surely Reece will get in even more trouble than us."

"When Reece thinks of something spiteful, he acts first and thinks through the consequences later," said Forge bitterly. "Anyway, his plan isn't going to work. I'll find another way out of here. There must be plenty more rooms with air vent inspection hatches in this area."

"I'm sure there are, but you won't be able to unlock the covers to get out."

"I'll just have to keep shouting through the grilles until I find a room where the owner is home, and ask him or her to let me out."

I choked. "Forge, you can't go round shouting through the air vent grilles of random teen rooms. I'm not sure how other boys would react to it, but a girl would think it extremely creepy behaviour. She'd be more likely to call Health and Safety to arrest you for spying on her than to let you out."

"You can't spy on people through these grilles," said Forge. "They're designed to stop anyone seeing through them."

"I doubt you'd have the chance to explain that."

Forge sighed heavily. "I'll have to find an inspection hatch in a corridor, or the shopping area, or some other public place then."

I considered that for a moment. "You'd be less likely to scare people that way, but shouting through a grille in a public place would attract a crowd."

"Instead of shouting, I could wait until late in the evening when no one was around, and message you to come and let me out. You wouldn't mind doing that, would you?"

I groaned. "I don't seem to have much choice."

"I'm really grateful," said Forge. "It may take me a while to find a suitable inspection hatch, and I'm getting a bit thirsty. My room has got one of the small air vents. Can you go down there, take the cover off, and pass me a few things?"

"What's your door code?"

"It's 12121."

I considered pointing out that 12121 wasn't much better than 54321 as a door code, but decided it wasn't worth it. "All right."

I went out into the corridor, and looked round suspiciously, but couldn't see any sign of Reece or anyone else. Two minutes later, I was in Forge's room. It looked oppressively neat compared to my room, and had three surfboards propped against the end wall next to the air vent grille. As I turned the catches and removed the small cover, I heard a shuffling sound, and then part of Forge's face appeared on the other side of the hole.

"You'd better charge my dataview so I can message you about my progress."

He passed me the dataview, and I plugged it into the charging point. "Why do you need three surfboards?"

"Two of them are old ones. Can you pass me the bottles of water from the shelf above the sleep field?"

I collected six bottles from the shelf. The labels said that they were specially enhanced water for professional athletes. "What's so special about this water?"

"Absolutely nothing. I bought a few bottles to impress the other teams in the swimming competitions, but the truth is that I keep refilling them with ordinary water."

I laughed and handed him the bottles. "Anything else?"

"The snack bars and the packet of crunch cakes from the same shelf. Oh, and the small backpack that's next to my swimming bag."

I had to squash the backpack flat to get it through the hole. There were loud rustling noises from the other side of the air vent. I guessed that Forge was loading everything into the backpack. I heard the dataview give the self-satisfied bleep that meant it had completed charging, and handed that through to Forge as well.

"I still think this is a bad idea," I said. "You have to be careful you don't get lost or have an accident."

"I've got a marker pen with me to number junctions. You'd better get me the other two marker pens from the drawer as well."

I fetched the marker pens. "If you haven't found your way out by ten o'clock this evening, I'm going to call Emergency Services."

"We can't give in that quickly." Forge gave me a pleading look through the air vent hole. "At least give me until tomorrow evening to find a way out."

I sighed. "All right, but then I'm definitely calling for help. Shall I put the vent cover back on now?"

"Don't worry about it," said Forge. "I'll fix it myself when I get out of here."

There was a scraping noise, a view of Forge's hair followed by a glimpse of backpack, and then he was gone.

I went over to the door, and looked out furtively. The corridor looked empty, so I hurried outside, but Shanna came out of her room at precisely the wrong moment. She gave me a confused look.

"Amber, I was looking for Forge. What were you doing in his room?"

I thought rapidly. "Forge had to go off somewhere unexpectedly. He asked me to take his swimming things back to his room."

"Oh." Shanna looked disappointed. "Where has he gone?"

"He didn't say." I tried to distract Shanna. "I was talking to Atticus a few minutes ago. He's asked me to be his partner for the Carnival parties."

"That's wonderful. Have you got your dress yet?"

"I was thinking of wearing the dress I wore last Carnival."

Shanna shook her head. "Even if that one still fits, you need something better to go to the couples' parties. I've made myself a new Carnival dress, so you can have my old one from last year."

"That would be wonderful."

"It will need a slight adjustment to the bodice, and the length shortening since I'm taller than you. Come along and I can alter it now."

"Just wait for one minute," I said. "I need to change my door code before I do anything else."

She frowned. "What? Why?"

"Because Reece worked it out and has been nosing in my room."

"Reece should be pelted with slime balls," said Shanna.

"Reece should be dropped head first into a slime vat." I hurried back to my room, started changing my door code, and hesitated. The new code had to be something that Reece wouldn't guess and Forge wouldn't find amusing. I punched in 77186.

CHAPTER TEN

"The idea is that you choose a door code you can remember," said the depressed man in an Accommodation Services uniform.

My morning wasn't going well. I'd stayed up late, waiting for Forge to call me to go and let him out of an inspection hatch, but heard nothing. I'd finally fallen asleep, fully dressed and sitting in a chair, and was woken by my dataview's alarm to find there was still no news from Forge.

I'd instantly pictured him falling down a lift shaft, and sent him a panicky message asking if he was all right. Forge had replied saying he was fine, it was just a bit more difficult than he'd expected to find a suitable inspection hatch, and could I refill the water bottles he'd left by the air vent in his room?

I'd cursed, but gone down the corridor to fill Forge's water bottles for him, which was how I'd got locked out of my room, and why I was being scolded by an irritated man from Accommodation Services.

"I'm sorry," I said. "I changed my door code yesterday evening. I could remember it last night, but I couldn't remember it this morning, so I had to call you for help."

He tapped at his dataview. "Name and identity code?"

"Amber 2514-0172-912." I recited wearily.

An image of me appeared on the dataview. The man stared at it, stared at me, and stared at the image again. "Yes, I think that's you."

"Of course that's me. Why would I lie about it?"

"Teens have been known to lie to try to get access to someone's room," he said gloomily. "I had one only yesterday. He claimed that..."

He broke off and stared at his dataview. "There's a behaviour monitoring alert on you."

"On me?" I squeaked. "Why?"

"Because you had a head injury two days ago." He frowned at me. "If you display signs of unusually severe headaches, confusion, abnormal behaviour, memory loss, or dizziness, you should be referred back to the medical facility that treated you."

"Oh, no, no, no. You can't send me back to Level 93 just because I forgot my door code. Teens must forget their door codes all the time."

The man tapped at his dataview. "You've never forgotten your door code before. Forgetting it now is an unusual memory loss."

"I've never *forgotten* my door code before because I've never *changed* my door code before. It's always been 54321, but a friend said that I should change it to something less obvious."

The man sighed. "I'll call the number on your medical discharge report and see what they say about it."

We'd already had an audience of Margot, Linnette and Preeja. Now Shanna arrived to join them, carrying a glittering silver dress over her arm.

"I've made the last alterations to your dress, Amber." She handed it to me. "What's going on here?"

"Amber forgot her door code," said Linnette, "and apparently she's supposed to go back to Level 93 for more treatment if she shows signs of memory loss."

"That's ridiculous," said Shanna.

"It's a sensible precaution," said Margot. "Amber's got a big bump on her head.

"I think that bump is mostly glue," said Preeja.

The man held his dataview to his ear. "Can the rest of you either leave or keep quiet? I don't need... Oh." His voice changed from impatient to official. "I've got a patient of yours here. Amber 2514-0172-912. She's forgotten her door code, and she's never done that before."

The man listened in silence for a moment, and then held out his dataview towards me. "Someone called Buzz wants to talk to you."

I took the dataview. "Hello, Buzz."

"Hello, Amber. How are you? Any symptoms other than forgetting your door code?"

"No, and I only forgot my door code because I'd changed it to something less easy to remember, so there's no need for me to go back to Level 93 to bother you again."

She laughed. "If you do need to see me again, then it wouldn't be at that Level 93 medical facility, Amber. I was just working there for the one day because their regular therapist was ill."

"Oh. Should I be talking to their regular therapist then?"

"No. I kept your case myself, since it just involved covering a few days of aftercare."

"I took your advice by the way."

"The bit about dating a boy? You've got a partner for Carnival?" Buzz sounded just as thrilled as Shanna by this news. "What's his name? Is he nice?"

I gave an embarrassed glance at my audience, retreated down the corridor, and whispered into the dataview. "The boy's name is Atticus, and I think he's nice. Shanna has given me a dress to wear."

"Is the dress like the one I told you I was going to wear for my deliciously handsome new neighbour?"

"The dress that was frighteningly respectable while dreadfully suggestive? No, this one is the dress Shanna wore for Carnival last year. It's spectacularly gorgeous. Much too spectacular for me really. Look!"

I held up the dress with one hand, and held the dataview away from me with the other, so I could send Buzz an image of the dress. When I held the dataview back to my ear, I heard her chatting away enthusiastically.

"It's definitely spectacular, but you'll look good in it. I adore the pink and silver sash trailing round the bodice." She paused for breath. "Do you remember me telling you about the boy I wanted to kiss on Teen Level?"

"The stunningly good looking boy?"

"That's the one."

I heard a pointed cough from next to me, and realized that the owner of the dataview had followed me down the corridor.

"I think we'd better stop chatting now," I said into the dataview. "The man from Accommodation Services is getting impatient."

"Tell him he should keep quiet when I'm evaluating my patient's condition," said Buzz.

I gulped. "I'd rather not tell him that."

"Then I'll tell him myself in a minute. Are you planning to copy my tactics to get Atticus to kiss you?"

I laughed. "You mean trap him in a lift? No, I don't think so."

Buzz's tone of voice abruptly changed from chatty to professional. "Your memory seems to be functioning perfectly, Amber. You don't just remember facts from two days ago, but you can repeat the exact phrases I used back then, and echo the tone of my voice when I said them. I hope you enjoy yourself at the Carnival parties. I'd like to talk to the man from Accommodation Services now."

I gave the man his dataview back. "Buzz wants to talk to you."

The man held the dataview to his ear. "Yes?" There was a long pause. "Well, it didn't sound like a memory test to me." There was another, much shorter pause, and he tapped the dataview to end the call.

"The medical staff are satisfied that you don't have any problems, Amber," he snapped at me. "I've reset your door code to the standard default code 11111. You should immediately change it to a new code. Please don't forget it again."

I didn't have time to reply before he stalked off down the corridor. I went back to join the others, and found them staring after the man.

"I think Buzz said something that annoyed him," said Preeja. "Who is Buzz anyway? A doctor?"

"Buzz is a Level 1 Psychological Therapist," I said. "She talks like an excited, chattering teen, but that may just be an act to make me relax and talk to her. I have a theory that she uses different acts for different patients."

Margot shrugged. "I expect a Level 1 Psychological Therapist is imprinted with lots of techniques for dealing with patients. Hurry up and change your door code now. We want to be at the community centre in time to eat breakfast before the morning activity session."

I groaned at the mention of the activity session, went into my room, hung the Carnival dress on a hook on the wall, and started changing my door code again. I daren't choose anything too clever this time. Forge's door code was 12121, so I punched in 23232.

Margot's voice shouted from outside my door. "Time to go, everyone!"

I went out into the corridor, and was greeted by a massed chorus of voices saying "Go away!" I recoiled in bewilderment, and then realized the order wasn't aimed at me but at Reece.

"I've as much right to go to the community centre and take part in activity sessions as the rest of you," said Reece.

"You've a right to go to the community centre," said Margot, "but you aren't walking there with us, and you aren't sitting at our table for breakfast either. If you try it, then Forge will..." She broke off and looked round. "Where is Forge? Is he skipping this activity session because he doesn't want to do embroidery?"

"I've just looked in his room, and he's not there," said Shanna. "Wherever he went yesterday, he's not back yet."

Of course Shanna would know Forge's room code and be bound to look in his room. I wondered if she'd noticed the air vent cover was missing. Probably not. She'd been looking for Forge, not inspecting the state of his room.

"Maybe Forge has moved to a room in a different corridor," said Reece maliciously. "I don't blame him if he has. I'd like to move myself. I've requested a room change three times, explaining how horrible you all are, but Accommodation Services keeps turning me down."

"Accommodation Services must have worked out that it's you that's horrible, not us," said Linnette.

"Forge would never ask to move room away from me," said Shanna. "He'd never leave his surfboards behind either. I'll call him."

She tapped at her dataview, and held it to her ear. "Forge, where the waste are you?"

I heard the faint murmur of Forge's voice answering her.

"So what level are you on," asked Shanna, "and when can I visit you?"

There was another murmur from Forge.

"And when will you be back? Please don't tell me that they're keeping you in for Carnival."

A final, very short, muttered comment from Forge.

Shanna sighed and put her dataview away. "Forge had an accident yesterday, and he's being treated in a medical facility."

"Not another one of us getting hurt," complained Preeja. "What's Forge done to himself, and why didn't he call us yesterday?"

I was keeping quiet to avoid lying to my friends. Forge had obviously based his story on my own accident. I hoped he hadn't claimed to have bumped his head, because that would be too much of a coincidence.

"He didn't call yesterday because he didn't want to worry me," said Shanna. "He says he's cut his leg, but it isn't serious. He thought they'd let him out this morning, but they've decided to keep him in a bit longer, and they're only allowing family to visit him. At least he's being treated on Level 16 instead of Level 93."

"If Forge is being treated in a Level 16 medical facility, then I can understand them not allowing visitors from Teen Level," said Atticus.

"We really need to go now if we want to have time for breakfast," said Margot pointedly. "You may be willing to eat one of those dreadful meals from your kitchen unit, but I'm not."

We moved off down the corridor. I glanced over my shoulder and saw Reece was watching us go with a sulky expression on his face. I wanted to yell at him for sneaking into my room, but I mustn't publicize the fact Forge was stuck inside the vent system.

Dealing with Reece would have to wait until either Forge had found his own way out or Emergency Services had rescued him.

When we reached the community centre, we found the usual range of breakfast food was on sale in one of the side rooms. We queued up to buy our meals and then gathered round one of the long tables at the back of the room. Atticus grabbed the chair next to me, while Shanna, Linnette and Preeja sat opposite us, grinning and exchanging whispers.

Atticus looked as if he wanted to talk to me but the audience was intimidating him. Margot was sitting on the other side of me, but she was fully occupied with her usual ritual of arranging everything on her plate into separate neat piles. I started eating myself, stabbing an egg viciously with my fork.

"What did that egg do to offend you, Amber?" asked Atticus.

"I'm picturing the egg being Reece."

Atticus laughed.

"It's not funny. If a telepath comes in here right now, and sees what I'm thinking about Reece, I'll get arrested."

"They'd have to arrest me as well," said Margot. "For that matter, why didn't a telepath arrest Reece years ago?"

"Telepaths can't possibly arrest everyone who has momentary angry thoughts, tells trivial lies, or commits acts of petty bullying." said Atticus. "If they did, they'd end up arresting half the people in the Hive. They have to focus their attention on people who are planning criminal acts that could harm others or damage the Hive."

I thought that over as I continued eating. Reece had trapped Forge in the vent system, and that had to qualify as an action that could harm him. Reece hadn't planned it in advance though. He'd discovered Forge was in there, and glued the inspection hatch cover in place on impulse. That meant there'd been no chance for a telepath to see the plan in Reece's mind and stop him, but a telepath could well read Reece's mind now and see what he'd done. If that happened, Reece would definitely get into trouble, but what about Forge and me?

"Time for the activity session." Linnette's voice interrupted my thoughts.

"Oh joy, oh rapture, oh unalloyed transports of delight," said Preeja glumly. "I don't know why I bothered coming. I already know that I'm dreadful at sewing."

Margot studied what was left on her plate, picked up a final salad leaf and ate it with a faint air of disgust, and then we all stood up and trooped through to room 8. I blinked in surprise, because the tables had been taken over by strange machines.

"I thought we were having another embroidery session," I said.

Our activity leader entered the room just in time to hear me. "This *is* another embroidery session, Amber. Last week, we did hand embroidery. This week, we're trying machine embroidery."

I decided that was good news. I'd found the slowness of hand embroidery stitching deeply frustrating. Machine embroidery wouldn't stop me making mistakes, but it would mean that I made the mistakes a lot faster.

Reece was already sitting at the back of the room, so I chose to sit at the front. Shanna sat at the table on my right, and Atticus on my left. The activity leader gave a brief demonstration of how to use one of the machines. I grimaced as I discovered this activity wasn't just about using a machine to embroider cloth, but also about creating the design in the first place. I was hopeless at anything creative.

The inevitable moment came when we had to attempt it ourselves. I dutifully set my machine to use several colours, fed in a piece of cloth, and sneaked a look across at Shanna. She was already running her machine, delicately trailing her fingers across the control screen to guide the design, and I saw her cloth start emerging covered with glorious blue and silver swirls that were highlighted with traces of purple.

I took a deep breath, started my own machine running, and tried to copy what Shanna was doing to guide the design. I was prepared for the result to be bad, but even so I was shocked by the discordant colours of the cloth that emerged. I'd been thinking about flowerbeds in parks when I chose red, purple and green, but somehow the colours that were bright and cheerful in a flowerbed looked garish on my cloth.

I glanced across at Atticus, and was even more depressed to see the cloth appearing from his machine was covered in a staid but perfectly acceptable design in blue and grey stripes.

"I'm useless," I muttered.

The activity leader appeared at my elbow. "There's no need to be despondent, Amber. This activity is only relevant to fabric designers."

I sighed. "It's not just this activity though. I'm useless at absolutely everything."

"You're a very competent swimmer," said the activity leader. "You may not have the height and build to achieve competition standard, but you still enjoy the benefits of high physical fitness. You've also got an exceptional sense of balance."

"I don't see how a good sense of balance will help me in Lottery."

"The Teen Level activity sessions are mainly focused around developing creative skills and sporting ability," said the activity leader, "but these are only relevant to a subset of the possible professions in the Hive. There are tens of thousands of other professions that involve basic innate abilities such as logical reasoning and social skills."

I must have heard activity leaders make a variation of this speech a hundred times by now. I listened in resigned silence as he continued.

"The assessment process is immensely complex, and its verdict is unpredictable, which is how it came to be named Lottery. Its tests will determine all your strengths, and you will be matched to the profession that is most suitable for you and valuable to the Hive, so you still have every chance of becoming high level."

His standard speech complete, the activity leader hurried off to help Casper feed the cloth into his machine and explain the controls again. I stared down at the horrible red, purple, and green disaster in front of me and groaned. In my first few years on Teen Level, I'd happily believed the activity leaders when they said that failing at the activities didn't matter, and that I still had every chance of becoming high level. Now the reassuring words just seemed like empty platitudes.

The painful session inevitably ended with our activity leader calling Shanna's name. He handed her a gold card, while the rest of us applauded. Shanna was my best friend, but I couldn't help thinking of how many gold cards she'd accumulated over the years, and how she openly admitted she didn't have time to attend even half of the advanced sessions.

It wasn't that I resented Shanna's good fortune, but it emphasized my own lack of talent. It was certain that Lottery would be sending me down the Hive; the only question was how far. I should be grateful if I ended up on Level 93, rather than as a Level 99 Sewage Technician.

CHAPTER ELEVEN

"You're very quiet," said Atticus, as we rode along on the express belt. "You didn't eat much lunch either. If you don't want to go on this date with me, Amber, then just admit it. We can forget the whole idea."

"I do want to go on a date with you," I said hastily, "but I find Light and Dark pageants a bit scary. Please don't laugh if I scream."

"I won't laugh. I get scared myself when the lights go out, especially during the pageants before Halloween when I know the dark forces will win. This is a Carnival pageant though, so we can reassure ourselves that light will triumph."

Carnival and Halloween were the twin Hive festivals of light and darkness, of life and death, and which force triumphed in the Light and Dark pageants reflected that. Other people were afraid of the periods of darkness, and the actors playing creatures from the Halloween stories, but my fears were centred on something else.

Explaining that to Atticus could get complicated, so I just nodded in response. We left the belt system, joined the vast queue outside the Blue Zone Arena, and eventually got inside.

I'd been to the arena dozens of times during my years on Teen Level. The arrangement of the interior varied depending on the event. This time there were no seats at all, only a long length of stage in the centre of the vast open space. Atticus and I were caught up in a crowd of other teens, and I found myself standing right next to the stage.

Atticus pulled a face at me. "I wasn't planning to get quite this close to the action. Do you want to move further away?"

I turned and saw a group of hasties were putting up white barriers to divide the audience into sections. "The crowd control safety barriers are already up, so we'd better stay where we are."

A few minutes later, the lights in the arena started dimming. There were terrified gasps from all around me as it gradually grew darker than the Hive corridors at night, darker than a park on the moon and stars programme, darker than the minimum room light setting, and on down to total blackness.

"It won't be dark for long," Atticus whispered tensely. "I can hold your hand if you're scared."

I felt his hand brushing against mine. "I'm not afraid of the dark," I said.

"Really? I thought everyone was afraid of the dark. Well, can I hold your hand because I'm scared?"

I giggled and took his hand. It felt oddly intimate to be standing so close together, with our hands linked in the darkness.

There was a sudden glow at the far end of the stage, as golden walls appeared that symbolized the Hive. The actress playing the light angel stood in front of them, her costume and outspread wings shining silver.

"Oh no," said Atticus. "They usually set up this end of the stage as the Hive walls, and the far end as Outside. They must have changed it this year. That explains why we ended up so close to the stage. The biggest crowds will be down the other end."

I bit my lip rather than try to speak. I wasn't scared of the dark, but I was terrified of the horrors of Outside.

The distant figure of the light angel brandished a glowing golden sword in defence of the Hive walls. "High up!" she cried.

"High up!" I joined in the answering shout of the audience.

Dark shapes were moving on our end of the stage now. Monstrous creatures with red glowing eyes. They made weird, high-pitched cries, which rose to a climax as a tall, cloaked figure wearing a red-eyed helm rose up from under the stage. There were squeals of panic from all around me. The hunter of souls, the nightmare central figure of all the Halloween stories, was here.

"Come to me, my cursed ones, my scavengers of darkness, my demonic pack," he called, in a harsh, distorted voice. "We will hunt souls this night and recruit them to swell our numbers."

He blew his hunting horn. The pack responded with inhuman cries, and loped across to gather round him. They acted out exaggerated sniffing, and led him across to the edge of the stage to be met with yells of fear from the audience. I peered sideways, and saw the crowd rapidly pulling back from the stage. The pack made snarling noises of frustration at losing their prey, before turning away to hunt an imaginary scent trail to further along the stage.

The act was repeated there, and a third and fourth time in other places, and then came the moment I'd been dreading. A glow was appearing almost in front of me. Truesun was rising up from under the stage!

I knew this wasn't the real Truesun that ruled the daytime outside the security of the Hive. It was just an actress in a costume, so I couldn't be blinded if I looked at it, but I was still terrified. I let go of Atticus's hand, and tried to move backwards, but the crowd was trapping me against the stage.

The glow grew brighter, and then a brilliantly lit golden headdress appeared. I had my eyes fixed on it, oblivious to anything else, until something touched my shoulder. I turned to see the hunter of souls looking down at me. In the light of the rising Truesun, I caught a glimpse of the actor's startled face under the red-eyed helm.

"Waste it! I must be losing my touch." He turned away, cowering and shading his eyes from the light of the rising Truesun, before running with his pack to hide in the darkest corner of the stage.

I realized I was standing alone in the centre of an empty space, and the nearby teens were all staring at me. I looked round for Atticus, and saw him standing a few paces back from the stage. He gave a nervous laugh and came back to my side.

"I thought you said you got scared during the Light and Dark pageants. I've never seen anyone stare straight into the eyes of the hunter of souls before."

"I'm not scared of the hunter of souls or his pack," I said. "I know they're just myths from Halloween stories. I'm scared of the Truesun, because that truly does exist outside the Hive."

I looked anxiously back at the stage. The Truesun was dancing round the stage in her dazzling headdress. As she moved towards me, I felt my heart start racing. I closed my eyes and pressed my face against Atticus's shoulder.

"You really are terrified," he said, in a bewildered voice, and put his arms protectively round me. "There's no need to worry. The actress playing the Truesun isn't going to risk coming near you after the way you faced the hunter of souls without flinching."

I didn't reply. I couldn't speak. I stayed with my eyes tight shut in the safety of the darkness and warmth of Atticus's shoulder. Finally, he spoke again.

"The Truesun has gone back under the stage. You're safe now."

"You're sure?"

"I'm sure," he said.

I turned to face the stage again, and cautiously opened my eyes. Yes, the Truesun had set, and the hunter of souls was back in the centre of the stage with his pack. They played at frightening the audience for a couple of minutes, and then a new figure appeared from under the stage. The dark angel, with his red and black costume, and his black wings outstretched, turned to face the audience and raised his red, glowing sword.

"Low down!" he cried, in a harsh voice.

The hunter of souls and his pack bowed to their champion, while the audience booed him. The dark angel waved his sword angrily at the crowd, and strode towards the golden walls of the Hive. The light angel came forward to meet him and blocked his path.

"We were lovers once," said the dark angel. "Join me in the darkness."

The light angel shook her head. "We were lovers once. Join me in the light."

The dark angel shook his head in turn, and then looked upwards. "I call for justice!"

A new figure, wearing unrelieved black and carrying a great sword on his back, was lowered down from the ceiling to stand between them. "You called for justice, and I am here. What is your plea?"

"Twice a year, I have the right to challenge those who banished me," said the dark angel.

"You have that right," said the figure of justice.

"Twice a year, I stand against his challenge," said the light angel.

"You also have that right. Let the combat begin."

Justice was lifted back up to vanish into the ceiling, and the two angels stepped forward. Their swords met with a loud clash, and they went through a dramatic combat routine that sent the hunter of souls and his pack scurrying clear of them.

At one point, the light angel was sent sprawling and lost her sword, but there wasn't any genuine suspense for the audience. We all knew that the dark angel would win in the pageants before Halloween, while the light angel would be victorious in the ones before Carnival.

The fight scene duly reached its climax, with the dark angel on his knees and the light angel's sword at his throat.

"Spare my life," pleaded the dark angel.

"Why should I spare you?" asked the light angel. "We are forever divided by our choices."

"We are forever divided, but forever one," said the dark angel. "There can be no light without darkness, and no darkness without light."

The light angel lowered her sword. "Go then."

The dark angel scrambled to his feet and fled, with the hunter of souls and the pack chasing after their defeated champion. They hurried down some stairs to vanish under the stage, and the light angel raised her sword in triumph.

"High up!" she cried.

"High up!" The crowd responded.

The light angel slowly paraded the length of the stage and back, celebrating her victory, and then the golden gates in the Hive wall opened. A group of people dressed in silver and gold came running out. "High up," they cried, and started tossing shimmering streamers to the crowd.

Eager hands reached up from the audience, grabbing for the streamers. I wasn't going to try to get a streamer myself, because taller people with a longer reach always got them first, but a silver-clad man came running up, knelt at the edge of the stage in front of me, and thrust a streamer into my hands. "Why didn't I scare you earlier?"

I stared at him in confusion, and then recognized his face and his voice as those of the hunter of souls. At Halloween, the dark angel would win the combat, and the hunter of souls and his pack would stay on stage and distribute red streamers to the crowd. Now I realized that at Carnival, those same actors would go under the stage for a rapid change of costume, and appear again as the victorious forces of light handing out silver and gold streamers.

"I was distracted by the Truesun rising," I said.

He looked puzzled, but the forces of light were gathering at the centre of the stage, and he stood and went to join them.

"Light is victorious," cried the light angel. "Let us go forth and tell the Hive to celebrate with Carnival!"

The light angel raised her sword high, and ran down the steps from the stage and through a gap in the crowd. The forces of light ran after her, cheering, and the waiting hasties moved forward to remove barriers so one section of the crowd after another was set free to chase after them in a long procession.

"High up!" we shouted, waving our streamers as we ran out of the Arena.

CHAPTER TWELVE

The light angel led the procession round a nearby shopping area, and through the local park, before stopping to climb on a park bench and flourish her sword. "Happy Carnival to you all, and may those of you entering the Lottery of 2531 all be high up!"

"High up!" the crowd responded for the last time, before turning and drifting back towards the nearby park exit. There was a major belt system interchange just outside, with a group of hasties making sure that the crowd formed an orderly line rather than all trying to get onto the belts at once. When Atticus and I had reached the head of the queue, and moved across to the express belt, Atticus turned to face me.

"I still don't understand why you're so scared of the Truesun."

The mere mention of the Truesun was enough to make me grumpy and defensive. "It's like my fear of heights. It's because of something that happened to me when I was a child."

"What happened to you?" asked Atticus.

Blurred memories of my infant terror surfaced. "It's hard to explain."

"I'll do my best to understand."

"When I say it's hard to explain, I mean that I hate talking about it," I snapped at him. "I've already told you I'm scared of the Truesun. Why can't you just accept that and shut up about it?"

Atticus lifted his hands in surrender. "I'm sorry. Let's talk about something else. Will you be going to the activity session tomorrow morning?"

"No. It's about making clay pots and I hate the feel of wet clay. I'm beginning to think I should give up going to activity sessions anyway. I'm used to being bad at them, but I was totally disastrous at this morning's machine embroidery. My cloth looked like it was covered in vomit."

"I was just as bad as you."

"Your design looked perfectly respectable."

"Only because I cheated," said Atticus.

"What? How could you have cheated?"

"I chose the minimum two colours, the totally safe ones of blue and grey, and I didn't touch the cloth design controls at all so it came out in the default stripes."

"Oh. I hadn't realized it worked that way." I hesitated for a moment. "Something funny happened on my way back from getting my head injury treated. I reached the bulkhead doors between Turquoise Zone and Blue Zone just as they closed for the three-monthly test, so I got stuck on the Turquoise side."

"I'm not seeing the joke," said Atticus.

"My head was hurting. I saw a set of chairs, so I went and sat down with some other teens."

"I'm still not seeing the joke."

"A Turquoise Zone activity leader arrived, and I discovered I'd gatecrashed his class's lecture on bulkhead doors."

Atticus laughed. "That reminds me of something that happened last year. Forge invited me to his swimming team party. When I arrived, nobody was dancing, and I couldn't see Forge or Shanna anywhere. The other peculiar thing was that everyone was tall and thin."

He paused. "I finally discovered I'd gone to the wrong community centre and walked into a meeting of the Blue Zone teen high jump team. I hope your activity leader wasn't as sarcastic about your mistake as the high jump team were about mine."

"The activity leader wasn't sarcastic at all. He thought my accident had stopped me from getting to my own class's lecture, and I was so desperately eager to learn about bulkhead doors that I'd decided to listen to his class's lecture instead."

"I expect it was very boring, but at least you got to sit down until the bulkhead doors opened."

"The lecture was so boring that I nearly fell asleep, but then the activity leader gave me a gold card for advanced sessions in engineering."

Atticus gave me a startled look and then smiled. "Amber, that's wonderful. Congratulations!"

"It isn't wonderful at all," I said glumly. "I was happily dozing when the activity leader called on me to answer a question. I'd no idea what he'd asked, so I picked a random label off a diagram, and it turned out to be right."

I waved my hands in despair. "After four years of hard work, I've earned one gold card for my swimming. Now I get handed a gold card for guessing an answer at random. I must be truly useless if I do better when I ignore lectures and guess answers."

Atticus pulled a sympathetic face. "You shouldn't worry so much about the Teen Level activity sessions, Amber. I go along to most of them because they can be interesting, but the reality is they'll have no effect on our futures at all."

I stared at him. "How can you say that?"

"Because it's true. We get the occasional activity session about things like engineering or hydroponics, but the overwhelming majority are about creative arts and sports. I worked out years ago that there's a good reason for that. Imprinted knowledge isn't enough for people who go on to work in those areas. Athletes need to do actual physical training, and artists need to develop their own individual creative style."

Atticus shrugged. "There may be other factors involved as well. It may be harder for Lottery to test for creative talents than other things, and the Hive wouldn't want to accidentally allocate a great artist or musician to work scrubbing slime vats. Anyway, my point is that you and I don't have an outstanding talent for creative arts or sports."

I sighed. "That's certainly true in my case."

"The activity sessions are set up to help the exceptional teens like Forge and Shanna. For the rest of us, they're just a way to keep us occupied and give us the comforting illusion that we have some control over our lives. The truth is that we don't."

Atticus pulled a grim face. "Nothing we do on Teen Level will make any difference to our future lives, Amber. Everything depends on what happens in Lottery. It will test our basic skills, and allocate us to whatever profession is most suitable for us and important to the Hive."

His expression abruptly changed to one of amusement. "If you think about it, there are some advantages in not having any particular talent. As everyone keeps telling us, the verdicts of Lottery are unpredictable. Shanna will be disappointed if she doesn't end up as a designer, and Forge has his heart set on becoming a professional athlete, but we'll enter Lottery with no preconceptions and be blissfully happy with whatever work it assigns us."

"Unless Lottery makes me a Level 99 Sewage Technician," I said gloomily.

Atticus made a choking noise. "I really don't think that's likely, Amber. You're a bright, articulate girl. Lottery is bound to find a more vital profession than Sewage Technician for you."

"I hope you're right about that, because..." I broke off and tensed. I could hear the distant sound of chanted numbers.

"Two ones are two."

"Two twos are four."

The sound was coming from ahead of us. There was a tall man in front of me, so I moved sideways to get a clear view. Yes, a telepath squad was standing further down the corridor, watching the people riding by on the belts.

"Two threes are six." I joined in the chanting. It was supposed to help stop the nosy from reading your thoughts. I didn't have anything to hide but... No, I did have something to hide. Forge was stuck in the vent system!

"Two fours are eight!" The people on the belt were shouting it now. I mustn't think about Forge. I tried to focus on the numbers. "Two fives are ten!"

The telepath squad was next to me now. The four hasties

didn't seem to be paying any attention to me, but I was sure the nosy was looking right at me.

"Two sixes are twelve."

"Two sevens are fourteen."

I was past the telepath squad. Nobody was calling my name or chasing after me. Chanting tables had worked. At least, I hoped it had worked. It was still possible that the telepath squad would turn up outside my room this evening.

Atticus was frowning at me. "I hadn't realized you were so terrified of nosies."

"Of course I'm terrified of nosies," I said. "Why weren't you chanting tables too?"

"Because there's nothing in my head that a nosy would care about," said Atticus. "I've probably got the most boring mind of all the five million teens on this level."

He gave me a teasing look. "Why are you so worried about a telepath reading your mind, Amber? Are you planning some horrific crime?"

I could feel myself flushing guiltily. "I just think nosies are horrible, creepy things. My parents and brother hate them too."

I wanted to escape from this conversation. I glanced at the overhead location signs. "I have to stop at the community centre to buy sandwiches."

"I'll come with you."

"There's no need for that."

Atticus grimaced. "Does that mean you don't want to go out with me again?"

"No, it means that seeing nosies upsets me, and I want to spend some time on my own to calm down." I sighed. "I'm scared of heights, the Truesun, and nosies. You must think me a total coward."

Atticus shook his head. "Nosies don't worry me, but they scare most people. Even Forge is a bit wary of them. There's nothing unusual in being scared of the Truesun either. I'm scared of it myself, but I'm even more scared of the dark and the hunter of souls, while those things don't seem to worry you at all."

He paused. "We'll be having another date then? Tomorrow perhaps?"

"Yes. I promised to help Shanna make Carnival streamers tomorrow morning, but we could go to the park in the afternoon. Linnette will be visiting her parents, and Casper will be at his learning support group, so we'll be able to spend some time with just the two of us."

"I'd like that," said Atticus.

I moved across to join the medium belt, and then the slow, before finally stepping off onto the corridor floor. Atticus turned to wave at me, and then the express belt carried him off into the distance.

I walked on down the corridor until I reached the community centre, and went inside to buy sandwiches for myself. As an afterthought, I bought extra sandwiches for Forge. I hadn't had any more messages from him, so he must still be in the vent system and getting hungry by now.

I knew I should be insisting that we called Emergency Services to rescue Forge, rather than encouraging him to stay in the vent system by buying him sandwiches. The problem was that I knew Forge just had to ask me to wait a little longer, and I'd give in as usual.

I walked back to my home corridor, let myself into Forge's room to put his sandwiches inside the air vent, and then headed back to my own room. As I reached my door, Shanna came walking down the corridor. I jumped nervously, hoping she hadn't seen me come out of Forge's room again. It would be hard to come up with an excuse for going in there a second time.

"Did your date with Atticus go well?" she asked.

"Reasonably."

"You don't sound very enthusiastic about it."

I sighed. "That's because we met a telepath squad on the way back. You know how much I hate them."

Shanna wrinkled her elegant nose. "I suppose that ruined your mood so Atticus didn't get the chance to kiss you goodbye. Are you having another date?"

"Yes. I'm seeing Atticus tomorrow afternoon."

"Good. Atticus is an attractive boy despite his low level parents." Shanna vanished back into her room.

I stared after her for a moment, stunned by that casual remark about Atticus's parents, then turned to punch in my door code. I tried to open the door, failed, and remembered I'd changed the code. Twice.

I punched in the correct 23232, went into my room, sat down, and frowned at the wall. How did Shanna know that Atticus had low level parents? I was sure that Atticus wouldn't have told her about them. He might have told Forge, since the two of them were best friends, but I didn't think that Forge would have passed on his friend's secret to Shanna.

I remembered Atticus saying it had been obvious who had high level parents when we first arrived on Teen Level. He'd noticed clues like the food and drink that we mentioned. Had Shanna noticed things as well? I could imagine her studying every detail of our parents' clothes and hair styles.

I'd often wondered why Shanna had chosen someone as insignificant as me to be her best friend. Atticus had said that Shanna's parents were elite, and I was the girl with the next highest level parents, while Forge had the highest level parents of the boys.

I had a sick feeling. Was this the reason Shanna had chosen me to be her best friend and Forge to be her boyfriend? No, of course not. It was horrible of me to consider the possibility. Shanna had chosen Forge to be her boyfriend because he was the most handsome boy on our corridor. She'd chosen me to be her best friend because she had a generous nature and could see I was feeling lonely and unhappy.

I dismissed my ridiculous suspicions, and took out my dataview. I sent a message to Forge, telling him I'd left some sandwiches inside the air vent, and asking if he'd found any inspection hatches yet.

Two minutes later, my dataview chimed with a message from Forge, thanking me for the sandwiches and saying he was going to collect them right away. He didn't mention anything about inspection hatches. I assumed that meant he either hadn't found any, or had found one but couldn't work out its location.

I could understand it was hard for Forge to tell where he was if he couldn't see anything through the grilles. He'd be dependent on sounds to give him clues. I was worried about letting him spend another night in the vent system though.

A possible solution occurred to me. I could tell Atticus about Forge being stuck in the vent system. I knew Atticus wouldn't wait around doing nothing for days when his best friend was in trouble. He'd either think of a clever way to rescue Forge or insist on calling Emergency Services.

The problem with involving Atticus was that I might get him in trouble as well. I sighed, munched my way through my sandwiches, and decided to lie down and listen to music.

I'd just turned on my sleep field, and stretched lazily out on it, when the lights went out. The cushion of warm air beneath me abruptly vanished, and I fell downwards, landing on my carpeted floor with a nasty thump.

CHAPTER THIRTEEN

I was lucky that my right elbow and hip took the brunt of my fall, so I didn't hit my injured head. I lay where I was for a moment, expecting the lights to come back on, but they didn't. I got to my feet, groped around to find my dataview, and used its glow to guide my way out to the corridor. That was pitch dark as well, except for the lights of other dataviews emerging from rooms.

I heard Margot's voice making the obvious remark. "It's not just the lights in my room then."

"Why did the lights go out?" asked the nervous voice of Casper.

"It's a power cut." Linnette was clearly trying to reassure Casper, but she sounded even more nervous than he did. "Don't you remember that we had a power cut three years ago? The lights were out for at least two minutes, and then suddenly came back on again. They'll do the same thing this time."

"Good," said Casper. "I don't like it being so dark."

Everyone gathered into a group, and waited restlessly for the power to return.

"Power Services usually fix things faster than this," muttered Preeja, from somewhere behind me. "Don't they know that our power is out? Should we call someone and tell them?"

"Power services have lots of monitoring systems," said Atticus. "They'll know we have a problem."

"I expect they've started their Carnival parties early and can't be bothered to help us," said Reece.

"They have to help us." Linnette's voice held a trembling note of panic now. "The Hive can't leave us in total darkness like this."

"Power Services will already be working to fix the problem," I said. "Ignore Reece. He's just trying to frighten us."

"I've no idea why you're all so scared of the dark," said Reece. "I like it. I suppose that's because I'm a naturally brave person and you're all cowards."

I heard a groan that I thought was from Atticus.

"The power could stay out for hours," added Reece. "Maybe even…"

"Shut up!" half a dozen voices shouted in unison.

"I'm just being realistic about… Ow! Who kicked me?"

There was another massed shout. "Shut up!"

Reece reluctantly went quiet. Several more minutes went by, with the tension steadily mounting. I wasn't scared of the darkness, but I was getting increasingly worried by the length of this power cut.

Three years ago, the power had gone off for two minutes. We found out afterwards that the power failure was caused by a teen in corridor 15. He'd been attending advanced sessions in electrical systems, did a little experimenting with the systems in his corridor, and took out all the power across corridors 1 to 20. That triggered an alarm in Power Services, and they rapidly got the power back on, though it took two days to stop the lights flickering in corridor 15.

I didn't dare to say it when Reece had already frightened everyone, but such a slow response from Power Services must mean something serious had happened. I was wondering if I should volunteer to go and see how many of the other corridors were without power, when Atticus spoke in a faintly embarrassed voice.

"The lights have been off for ten minutes now, and we haven't received any messages from Emergency Services telling us what to do, so I'm taking charge of the situation."

"You're taking charge of the situation?" Shanna sounded both scared and angry. "Who do you think you are?"

"I think I'm this corridor's emergency warden."

"No, you aren't," said Shanna. "Forge is our corridor's emergency warden. Since he isn't here, I'd better take charge myself."

"Forge is our corridor's emergency warden," snapped Atticus. "I'm his deputy. Since Forge isn't here, I'm taking charge, and I am officially requesting you to stop arguing, Shanna. Forge and I have been on the warden training courses. I know what to do. You don't."

"I didn't know that you'd been on the warden training course with Forge," said Shanna ungraciously. "You should have said that to start with. Carry on then."

"Thank you, Shanna," said Atticus bitterly. "Now, listen carefully everyone. Hive protocols state that after ten minutes without power, in the absence of other instructions from Emergency Services, the local emergency warden should take charge of the situation and initiate first response protocols."

He paused. "First response step one is to secure our lighting. Will Amber and Margot please follow me to our emergency store room?"

"I'd be happy to follow you," said Margot, "but which dataview are you?"

One of the dataviews was held higher up and waved in the air. "I'm this one."

The dataview headed off down the corridor. Margot and I elbowed our way through the crowd to follow it. By the time we caught up with Atticus, he was punching a code into the store room door. He opened it, went inside, there was a clanking sound, and a light came on. It was only a lantern rather than a proper room light, but it seemed shockingly bright after the darkness.

Atticus came out, and I saw the lantern was a more functional version of the ones people carried when they were in Halloween costumes. Atticus handed the lantern to Margot, went into the room again, and started passing out more lanterns to us.

"You wind the small handle on the side ten times to start the lanterns working. There should be enough for one each."

Everyone else had followed us down the corridor by now, attracted by the lights. "Why do we have to wind the handles?" asked Casper, studying his lantern in fascination. "We don't do that with Halloween lanterns."

"These lanterns don't have power cells like the Halloween ones," said Atticus.

Casper started enthusiastically winding up his lantern.

"That's enough, Casper," Atticus hastily intervened. "It only needs ten turns. After that, you wait until the light starts flickering, and then wind the handle another ten times."

"These lanterns are primitive," complained Reece.

"Using our dataviews as lights will drain their charge fast, and we've no way to recharge them," said Atticus. "These lanterns may seem primitive, but they'll keep working indefinitely. I suggest we all set our dataviews to power conservation mode now."

Everyone adjusted their dataviews.

"First response step two is a roll call." Atticus started calling out names.

The roll call showed everyone in our corridor group was here except Forge. He must still be stuck in the vent system. I hoped he was far enough away for the vent system lights to still be working.

"First response step three is to secure our water supply," said Atticus. "Margot and Linnette, I'm putting you in charge of doing that. The big box on the store room floor contains twenty-four collapsible water storage bottles. The…"

He was interrupted by a chorus of chimes from dataviews. I grabbed mine from my pocket and saw a message from Emergency Services. Several voices read it aloud.

"Your area is currently experiencing a power outage. Power Services are aware of the situation and are working to restore power. You should obey the instructions of your nearest emergency wardens and report any problems to them. Do not make any calls or send messages, as the communication system in your area must be kept clear for Emergency Services. People trapped in lifts should call Emergency Services and be prepared to give their lift number, the approximate floor number where it stopped, and the number of people in the lift."

"Hopefully it won't be too long before they fix the problem." Linnette sounded much more cheerful now that we had the lanterns working and a message from Emergency Services. "I'm so thankful that I'm not stuck in a lift."

I pictured being trapped in a lift with a crowd of frightened people, or worse still a telepath squad, and nodded my heartfelt agreement.

"To continue what I was saying," said Atticus, "the water supply pumps will have stopped working when the power went out, but there'll still be water in storage tanks. Margot and Linnette, you should go round the taps in our corridor, and fill as many bottles as possible. They'll expand to full size when you fill them. Pick some people to carry the bottles to our community room."

"Do we really need to store water?" asked Reece. "The power will probably come back on in a minute."

"It's better to store the water and not need it, than the other way round," said Atticus. "Now our corridor belongs to an emergency group of ten corridors. While you're securing the water supply, I need to go and report our status to our emergency group leader, and see if any of the corridors of younger teens need help. Since Forge isn't here, I'm making Amber my deputy, so she'd better come with me."

"Why are you making Amber your deputy instead of me?" Shanna sounded offended.

"Because Amber hasn't been arguing with me. We'll be back in a few minutes."

Atticus and I carried our lanterns down to the end of the corridor. "You have to make allowances for Shanna," I said. "She's in a bad temper because she's terrified of the dark."

"We're all terrified of the dark," said Atticus. "Well, everyone except you and Reece. Frankly, I wish that Reece was scared of the dark too. If he starts trying to frighten people again, I'll do more than kick his ankle."

I blinked. "It was you that kicked Reece? I assumed it was Margot."

"As emergency warden, it's my duty to take all necessary measures to prevent panic," said Atticus. "Reece was lucky. Margot would have kicked him a lot harder than I did."

I giggled.

We turned the corner into a wider corridor with a slow belt running along it. There was no sign of light in either direction, and the belt was still and lifeless. Atticus stopped walking and took two objects from his pocket. They looked vaguely like the bulky, basic dataviews used by small children.

"Aren't we going to the emergency group leader's corridor?" I asked.

"No, we're going to call in using these emergency communicators, but we don't want the rest of our corridor group listening to us."

"You think something has gone seriously wrong?" I asked anxiously.

"I *know* something has gone seriously wrong," said Atticus. "We should have got a much faster and more detailed message from Emergency Services."

He handed me one of the communicators. "These have handles to wind like the lanterns, and a white button that turns them on and off. They display incoming messages from Emergency Services, and you can use them to talk to the other wardens in your emergency group. You can hear what other people are saying at any time, but if you want to say something yourself, then you have to hold down the green button."

Atticus wound the handle on his communicator, and its screen came to life, showing the same message we'd all had on our dataviews. "Waste it! Emergency Services haven't even sent out extra information on the warden network. What's going on?"

He didn't seem to expect me to reply to that, because he held down the green button and spoke into the communicator. "Corridor 11 checking in. This is Atticus speaking. Twenty-one people present. Forge is away having treatment in a medical facility, so I've deputized a girl called Amber to help me. First response step three is in progress."

"Thank you, corridor 11," said a female voice. "I'm now just waiting for corridor 15 to report. If they don't do that in the next two minutes, someone will have to go there and find out what's happening."

"Is that Ruby from corridor 12?" Atticus sounded startled. "You're emergency group leader?"

"I'm *acting* emergency group leader," she said, with a heavy emphasis.

Atticus frowned but released the green button without saying anything else.

"Corridor 15 here," said a breathless, young, male voice. "Sorry I'm late, but Rufus had a panic attack. He's scared of the dark. Well, everyone's scared of the dark, but Rufus is…"

"Can you give us a situation report, corridor 15?" Ruby's voice interrupted him.

"Oh yes, this is Jaime speaking. My deputy is here too. Sixteen people present in our corridor. First response step three is in progress."

"Thank you, corridor 15," said Ruby. "Eight corridors have now reported at least one warden present and first response step three in progress. The other two corridors are totally empty, because all the eighteen-year-olds have gone off to a Lottery candidates' event in a different area. That's left us with a hundred and thirty people, twelve trained wardens, and no emergency group leader. My deputy, Pippa, has been organizing our corridor while I filled in as emergency group leader."

She seemed to hesitate. "Atticus, you're the only other seventeen-year-old warden present. Are you happy with me continuing as acting emergency group leader?"

Atticus briefly pressed the green button again. "Definitely. You're filling the role far better than I would."

"All right then," said Ruby. "Listen closely, everyone. We're supposed to wait for instructions from Emergency Services, but we're approaching the half hour mark now, and we've still only received a standard message. That must mean there's a major power problem, and I want some idea of how big an area has been hit."

She paused. "I'm going to break protocol and ask you to

message a family member to find out if the power is still working where they are. We mustn't do anything to spread panic, so just say you've heard there's a power outage and want to know if they're all right. I'll wait a few minutes for you to do that, and then ask for updates."

I looked at Atticus. "Should we really do this? Emergency Services said we shouldn't send messages."

"Ruby is our emergency group leader, so we obey her orders," said Atticus. "I agree with her anyway. We need to know the extent of this."

I took out my dataview. My parents were on Level 27, so they should be well away from the power outage, but they'd be horrified at me disobeying instructions and sending them a message. I took the safer option of messaging my brother, Gregas.

The response from Gregas came a minute later. "Dad says you should know better than to message us when our power is out."

"Thank you very much, Gregas," I muttered bitterly. I'd get a lecture from my parents next time I spoke to them, but I was more worried by the fact the power was out on Level 27.

Atticus turned to me. "The power is out on Level 80."

"It's out at my parents' apartment too."

A couple of minutes later, Ruby's voice came from the communicator. "I'll try not to pry into anyone's home level. Does anyone have a report of the power out somewhere?"

Atticus held down the green button. "Yes."

I leaned over to speak into the communicator myself. "Yes."

There was a ragged chorus of other people saying yes, and Ruby groaned. "Does anyone have a report of the power *on* somewhere?"

There was dead silence until Ruby spoke in a grim voice. "I'm assuming you all messaged family members at home, so that means they're on a random range of Hive accommodation levels, but all in areas vertically above and below us."

A young girl's voice spoke. "I messaged my mother, and she was at work on Industry 3."

That was followed by the voice of an older boy. "My father was at work on Industry 41."

Ruby sounded even grimmer now. "It sounds as if the power is out in area 510/6120 on every level of the Hive, from Level 100 right up to Industry 1. Now we need to know how far the power outage extends horizontally. If anyone knows the numbers of people in other areas of Blue Zone, please call or message them now."

"Forge is on the Blue Zone teen swimming and surfing teams," said Atticus, "so he must know the numbers of team members from all across Blue Zone, but I don't know anyone outside this area. How about you, Amber?"

I shook my head. "I've only got the number for the Level 1 Psychological Therapist that treated me after my accident, and she's far away in Turquoise Zone."

A tense voice spoke from the communicator. "The power is out in area 230/6910."

I caught my breath. Area 230/6910 was a vast distance away, right on the other side of Blue Zone.

The next voice wasn't just tense but shaking from fear. "Jason here. Power outage in area 840/6080."

"Try to stay calm, Jason." Ruby was obviously struggling to stay calm herself. "The power outage is very widespread then, probably affecting the whole of Blue Zone. Does anyone know the numbers of people in other zones of the Hive?"

There was total silence. Where possible, Lottery assigned people to work in their home zone, so few people would have family members in other zones. Atticus pushed the green button. "Amber has the number of a Level 1 Psychological Therapist in Turquoise Zone."

"Call the number," said Ruby. "We need to know if the other zones of the Hive, especially the ones next to us, still have power."

I gave Atticus a panicky look. "I can't casually call someone that's Level 1!"

"Amber, you haven't had emergency warden training," said Atticus. "You don't understand how bad this situation could be. If a power outage is this widespread, and lasting this long, then we need to start worrying about our air supply."

I gasped. We'd had lessons in school about how the reclaimed water and stale air were purified on Level 100. Atticus had pointed out earlier that the power cut would have stopped the pumps that supplied our water. I'd realized that meant the fans in the vent system would have stopped as well, but vaguely assumed that fresh air would still drift in from neighbouring corridors.

If the whole of Blue Zone was without power, then there wouldn't be any fresh air arriving here at all. When we'd used up all the oxygen...

"How long will our air last?" I asked urgently. "Is there anything we can do to...?"

"There isn't time for me to explain the emergency systems now," interrupted Atticus. "We need to know if Turquoise and Navy Zones still have power. Call your therapist."

CHAPTER FOURTEEN

My fingers trembled as I looked up my medical discharge record on my dataview, and called the number. I was relieved when the call was answered, and then terrified by the fact it was a sound only connection. Buzz must have her dataview in power conservation mode too. That was a bad sign. A very bad sign.

I moistened my lips. "Buzz, it's Amber. Is your power on?"

"Hello, Amber." There was an oddly wary note in Buzz's voice. "Why are you calling to ask me that?"

"There's a power outage here. We know the power is out across the whole of Blue Zone, and my emergency group leader told me to call you and ask if the power in Turquoise Zone is still on." It was probably obvious from my voice, but I said it anyway. "I'm scared. We're all scared."

"Ah, yes. I'd forgotten you lived in Blue Zone." Buzz paused as if she was thinking something through. "There's been a delay in sending out information because it takes time to assess a situation on this scale. You should get an update soon, but if you've already worked out the power outage covers all of Blue Zone, then it's perfectly understandable that you're scared, so I'll give you some details now."

She paused again. "There's been a failure of power supply nexus 7. That took out all the power for Blue Zone. The Hive is designed to have an independent power supply for each zone, so none of the others are affected by the power outage. The safety systems have triggered an automatic closure of the Blue Zone bulkhead doors, but there's absolutely no need to worry."

No need to worry? The other night, I'd watched a test closure of the great bulkhead doors. Now those bulkhead doors had closed on Blue Zone again. We were cut off from the rest of the Hive and running out of air!

Buzz must have heard my instinctive moan of fear, because she repeated her words in a soothing voice. "There's absolutely no need to worry. Tell your emergency group leader that the repair work will take time, but Turquoise and Navy Zones have power, and Oasis is already operating."

I didn't know what Oasis was, but I clung to the reassuring fact that Turquoise and Navy Zones had power. The Hive worked together for the good of all. Turquoise and Navy Zones would find a way to help us. They had to help us. Once the air ran out, my friends would die, my family would die, and I'd die myself.

Buzz was still speaking. I tried to blot out my nightmare visions of ten million people struggling to breathe, and focused on what she was saying.

"Health and Safety are sending teams through the bulkhead emergency access routes from both Turquoise and Navy Zones to assist with lift rescues and other problems. I'm part of the medical support on one of those teams."

"You're coming into Blue Zone yourself?" I was stunned.

"I'm in Blue Zone right now, Amber. That's why I've got my dataview set to take calls on sound only to conserve power. I have to go now. My team has just got some lift doors open, and I have patients to help."

"I understand. Thank you." I ended the call.

"What did she say?" demanded Atticus.

"She…"

"No, don't just tell me, tell everyone."

Atticus held down the green button on his communicator, and I leaned over to speak into it. "Buzz said that something important in the power supply has failed. I think she said it was a nexus. Anyway, that's taken out all the power for Blue Zone, and our bulkhead doors have closed, but the rest of the Hive is fine.

Buzz said to tell you that repair work will take time, but Turquoise and Navy Zones have power, and something called Oasis is already operating."

Ruby's voice spoke. "You said this Buzz person was a Level 1 Psychological Therapist. She'd naturally know if the power is on where she is, but how would she know the status of Oasis?"

"Buzz said Health and Safety are sending teams into Blue Zone through the bulkhead emergency access routes, and she's on one of those teams."

"Your therapist works for Health and Safety." Ruby gave a relieved sigh. "That means we can trust her information on Oasis. If that's already operating, the situation isn't critical, but we should be prepared to implement second response protocols and…"

Jason's panicking voice cut in.

"Turquoise Zone has power and air. We should forget second response protocols and start walking north immediately. We're at 510/6120, and we only need to get to 510/5999."

"You're seriously suggesting we try walking to Turquoise Zone, Jason?" asked Ruby. "It may not seem far to 510/5999 when you're whizzing along on an express belt, but it's a very long way on foot through a maze of pitch-dark corridors."

"Those corridors can't be any darker than the one I'm standing in now," said Jason.

"You're standing in a dark corridor that you know very well," said Ruby. "We'd soon get lost in a strange area. Even if we didn't, how many hours would it take us to walk to the bulkhead between Blue and Turquoise Zones, and what would we do when we got there? All the bulkhead doors are closed. If you know how to find the emergency access routes through the sealed bulkhead and reach Turquoise Zone, then please tell me, because I don't."

She waited but there was no reply from Jason. I ruefully remembered dozing through that lecture on the bulkhead doors. If I'd paid attention back then, I'd probably know all about emergency access routes.

"We're going to forget about walking to Turquoise Zone, and put our trust in the Hive," Ruby continued. "We know that Oasis is already operating. At some point in the next couple of hours, we should be told to move to the park."

"Can't we move to the park right away?" It was a girl's voice.

"No, we can't," said Ruby firmly. "Remember your warden training. If everyone tries to move through pitch-dark corridors at once, people will get injured. Top priority areas, like childcare and medical facilities, evacuate to the park first. Then public places like shopping areas. Then corridor blocks get instructed to move in turn."

"But what if there's a mistake, and we don't get our instructions?" It was Jason talking again. "At the four hour point, we'll start noticing the first symptoms of..."

"There's no need to worry about that," Ruby interrupted him. "If we don't hear anything by the two hour point, I'll give the order to move myself."

She paused. "Now get back to your corridors, and warn your friends that the power will be out for a while. You mustn't let them know how big an area is affected. Don't say a word about the air issue either. People are already scared, and we don't want to tip them over the edge into panic. I'll be listening in to the group circuit on my communicator at all times, so you can tell me if you have any problems."

Atticus put his communicator in his pocket and picked up his lantern.

"What is Oasis," I asked, "and why will we be moving to the park?"

"Oasis is the Hive emergency system where neighbouring zones supply power and air to a zone that's in trouble," said Atticus. "Turquoise and Navy Zones can't supply everywhere in Blue Zone without risking overloading their own systems, so the Oasis network only supplies the neighbourhood parks. Right now every park in Blue Zone has power, fresh air, and a lake full of water that can be filtered and drunk."

There'd be fresh air in the park! I'd thought the Hive parks were places for children to play, adults to relax, and people to hold parties. I hadn't realized they were also a vital part of the Hive emergency system.

My friends and I just needed to reach our local park and we'd be safe. There'd be emergency wardens on Level 27, making sure my parents and Gregas made it to safety as well. I felt dizzy with relief, but then I remembered the person who wouldn't be able to make it to a park, and tensed again.

"If Oasis will only supply air to the parks, then I need to tell you about Forge. He's not in a medical facility, but…" I broke off and frowned. "I think I can hear someone shouting. Is that Reece's voice?"

CHAPTER FIFTEEN

Atticus groaned and started running. I chased after him. As we turned the corner into our corridor, I could see a group of lanterns standing on the floor. Silhouetted against their light, several figures were shouting at each other, while more were huddled together on the far side of the lanterns. When they saw us coming, they all instantly stopped shouting at each other, and started shouting at Atticus instead.

"Finally!"

"You've been ages."

"You said you'd be away a few minutes, not hours."

"Did you really think this was a good time for you two to go off and cuddle each other?"

The shouts all came at once, so I wasn't sure who'd said what, except that I was pretty sure that the remark about cuddling had come from Reece.

"Quiet!" yelled Atticus.

There was a grudging silence.

"We needed to get full information on what was happening and decide the best way to handle the situation," said Atticus. "I thought that if the fourteen-year-olds could wait patiently for their corridor wardens to do that, then seventeen-year-olds could be trusted to do the same, but I was obviously wrong."

"It was Reece's fault," said Margot bitterly. "First he laughed at us for being afraid of the dark, and then he started telling Halloween stories."

"He said that now there were no lights, the hunter of souls could bring his demon pack in here to hunt us." Linnette's voice was shaking.

"That can't be true." Casper gave her a reassuring pat on the shoulder. "We're safe inside the Hive."

"Of course we're safe inside the Hive," I said. "Reece was telling lies to frighten you."

"That's not nice," said Casper.

"No, it isn't," said Shanna forcefully. "Reece isn't nice. In fact, Reece is a useless piece of slime."

"For once, I totally agree with you, Shanna," said Atticus. "If Reece causes any more trouble, I'll tie him up and gag him."

"You've got no right to threaten me," said Reece.

"Actually, I do," said Atticus. "In an emergency, wardens have the right to take any and all measures necessary to stop someone inciting panic."

"Forget Reece," said Shanna. "When is the power going to come back on?"

"You should all be getting an information update on your dataviews soon," said Atticus, "but the basic situation is that something big went wrong in the power system. Repair work has started, but it will take some time to fix it."

"How long is some time?" asked Preeja. "It's creepy only having lanterns for light."

"I'm getting hungry too," said Casper. "My kitchen unit isn't working, and I don't want to go to our community centre to buy food when everywhere is so dark."

"I doubt that the community centre will be selling food now anyway, Casper," said Atticus, "but we have a stock of emergency ration bars. I'll get those out in a minute, but I want you all to pack a bag first. At some point in the next hour or two, we'll be getting instructions to move, so we need to be packed and ready to go."

"Move? Why would we be told to move somewhere else?" asked Shanna. "It's bad enough standing here in the dark. We don't want to be groping our way along strange corridors with nothing but a few lanterns."

"We'll be told to move because the lights aren't working here," said Casper happily. "If it's going to take a long time to mend them, then the Hive will send us somewhere that the lights do work."

"That's exactly right, Casper," said Atticus. "We'll be moving to somewhere with working lights. Now everyone should pack one bag with the bare essentials for a couple of days. Ideally that bag should be a backpack, because we'll need to carry the bottles of water, the lanterns, and all the other emergency supplies as well."

"Days?" Shanna said, in outraged tones. "This can't drag on for days. What about our area Carnival celebrations? I'm on the entertainment committee, and we've been working on the preparations for weeks!"

"I'm sure that Power Services will be doing their best to fix the problem before Carnival."

Atticus sounded as if he was on the edge of losing his temper. I couldn't blame him for that. We had far more important things to worry about than Carnival parties. Jason had said the air would start going bad at the four hour point. I kept trying to calculate how much time we had left, and fretting about Forge being trapped in the vent system.

In fairness, Shanna didn't know about the air issue, and we couldn't explain it to her. Ruby had been quite right that any mention of air problems could trigger mass panic.

"Everyone go and pack your bag now," said Atticus. "Be back here in fifteen minutes."

The others hurried off with their lanterns. Atticus watched them go, then gave a low groan and sagged against the wall.

"Are you all right?" I asked.

"No, I'm not all right." Atticus groaned again. "We had training sessions in dark corridors during our warden training, but I knew they'd only last for twenty minutes. It's so much harder coping with the darkness when you know it could last for days."

He paused. "I'm supposed to stay calm and set a good example to the others, but the truth is that I feel like the walls are closing in on me. There's the shadow issue too. Have you noticed the way the light from the lanterns casts weird shadows that seem to move for no reason?"

"Not really, but I'm not scared of the dark."

Atticus ran his fingers through his hair. "I should never have let Forge talk me into being his deputy warden, but it seemed so unlikely that we'd ever have a genuine emergency. Even if we did, I assumed Forge would be here to take charge. It was obvious in training that he was much better than me at coping with the darkness."

"About Forge," I said. "I'm afraid he lied to Shanna when he said he was at a medical facility."

"You mean that Forge went off to some multi-day swimming event? I expect he realized Shanna would be angry about him vanishing for days just before Carnival, so he lied to avoid an argument."

"No," I said miserably. "Forge lied because he'd gone exploring in the air vent system."

"What?" shrieked Atticus. "Waste that!"

I made desperate hand gestures to indicate that Atticus shouldn't shout that loud. "I told Forge it was a bad idea, but he insisted. He said it would be exciting."

"I'll have a few exciting words to say to him when he gets back," said Atticus grimly. "I'm Forge's best friend, and he didn't tell me about this. Shanna is his girlfriend, and he didn't tell her about it either. Why did you get dragged into it?"

"Because the only vent system inspection hatch in our corridor was in my room."

"You should have refused to let Forge tamper with it."

"I would have refused if he'd bothered to ask my permission, but he didn't. He sneaked into my room while I was at the medical facility on Level 93. The first I knew about it was when I opened my door. Forge appeared out of the hole in my wall, dressed in black, and wearing a headband with lights attached to it. I was scared to death."

"So that's why you changed the door code for your room," muttered Atticus.

"Yes. Forge insisted on going back into the vent system when I went to visit my parents yesterday, and as far as I know he's still in there."

"He must have come out by now. Even Forge wouldn't want to stay in the vent system for over twenty-four hours."

"He didn't want to stay in there that long, but Reece glued the hatch cover shut in my room."

"You mean Reece trapped Forge in the vent system? Why didn't Forge call Emergency Services to rescue him?" Atticus shook his head. "No, don't bother answering that. I can guess the reason. Forge was too proud to ask for help."

"He thought he could find another inspection hatch and call me to help him get out."

"Finding another inspection hatch must have turned out to be harder than Forge expected."

"I think the problem may not have been finding an inspection hatch, but working out its location. Apparently the vent system is very confusing, and you can't see anything through the grilles of the inspection hatch covers."

Atticus sighed. "Whatever the problem was, Forge must be getting hungry and thirsty by now."

"He got me to go into his room and put some food and drink inside the little air vent there." I waved a hand in dismissal. "The food and drink doesn't matter. It's Forge's air supply that's critical. We can get to the park, but he can't."

"Forge's air supply shouldn't be an issue," said Atticus. "Once all the thousands of teens in our area are in the park, there'll be plenty of air left for the remaining few emergency workers, the people trapped in lifts, and the occasional fool like Forge."

I thought that through and calmed down a little. "That's true, but I still think we should call Emergency Services to come and rescue him."

"There's no point in calling Emergency Services," said Atticus. "They won't come and help."

"Of course they will. It's their job."

"There are one hundred million people in our Hive, Amber.

Ten million of them in Blue Zone. How many people do you think are trapped in lifts right now? Ten thousand? Twenty thousand? More?"

"Maybe," I said uneasily.

"Now imagine you're an Emergency Services coordinator overloaded with calls for help. Are you going to send one of your teams to search for a boy who'd chosen to take the risk of exploring the vent system, or to free a dozen travellers stuck in a lift through no fault of their own?"

I didn't like what Atticus was saying, but I could see his point.

"We don't even know where Forge is," added Atticus. "As soon as we've packed our bags, we'll call him and see if he's got any idea of his location."

"I'd rather call him now."

"It's my responsibility to get our corridor group ready to move to the park, and that includes the two of us," said Atticus firmly. "We pack our bags, and then we call Forge."

I hurried to my room, tipped my swimming gear out of its backpack, and threw in some clothing and a few other oddments. When I went out into the corridor again, almost all of our group were there. Most of them had followed instructions and brought one backpack. A few had bigger shoulder bags or hand luggage.

"We seem to be missing Shanna," said Atticus. "Can you go and help her pack, Amber? If humanly possible, can you please limit her to one bag that isn't…"

He broke off. Shanna had finally arrived. She was carrying one shoulder bag, which was large, but not ludicrously so. There was a flurry of chimes from dataviews. We finally had another message from Emergency Services.

Margot read it aloud. "Power Services are still working to restore power to your area. You will soon be asked to implement second response protocols. Your emergency wardens will instruct you in how to prepare for this. Please remain patient and obey their instructions promptly."

"We might as well eat while we're waiting," said Atticus.

He did some grovelling in the back of the emergency store

room, brought out what looked like packets of crunch cakes, and handed them round. I ripped one open, bit into it, and frowned. Casper put my thoughts into words.

"This isn't a very good crunch cake."

"I'm afraid that emergency ration bars don't taste very nice, but they're all we've got," said Atticus. "Amber and I have another job to do now. We'll be back in a few minutes."

"How long is the few minutes going to be this time?" asked Reece.

"Hopefully a lot shorter than last time."

Atticus and I walked off down the corridor with our lanterns. I glanced over my shoulder, and saw Casper was munching his ration bar philosophically, while everyone else stood around watching him. I wasn't sure if they were checking to see if he survived without being poisoned, or just delaying the evil moment of having to eat their own ration bars.

"Casper's coping with this far better than I'd have expected," I said.

"Casper trusts the Hive to take care of him," said Atticus. "In the current situation, that effectively means he's trusting *me* to take care of him. I just hope that I don't let him down."

We stopped at the end of the corridor. I took out my dataview, set it to speaker mode so Atticus could join in the conversation as well, and called Forge.

"Hello, Amber," he said.

"Forge, where are you?" I asked. "Do you realize the power is off?"

"Oddly enough, I realized the power had gone off when the lights went out," said Forge. "If Emergency Services are sending out instructions to implement second response protocols, then Power Services are obviously going to take several hours to fix things, but there's no need to worry about me. I've got food and water, and the lights on my headband will keep working for at least another ten hours, so I can wait where I am until the power is back on."

Atticus leaned over to speak into my dataview. "Excellent plan, Forge. Just one slight problem with it. The power is out across the whole of Blue Zone, and it will take days rather than hours to do the repair work."

There was a pause before Forge answered in a tense voice. "That's a bit... awkward. What about Oasis?"

"Oasis is operating," said Atticus.

"Then there isn't really a problem," said Forge. "It won't be pleasant when the lights in my headband stop working, but I'll cope somehow."

"Of course there's a problem," I said. "We have to get you out of the vent system right now. Whereabouts are you?"

"I've no idea."

Atticus leaned across to join in the conversation again. "Are you saying you don't know because you're too proud to admit you need help, or because you've genuinely no idea where you are?"

"I've genuinely no idea where I am. When the power cut out, I was exploring an area of the vent system that had motion-triggered lighting. I was halfway down a ladder when everything went totally black."

"Halfway down a ladder!" I echoed his words in horror.

"Yes, and I couldn't use my headband lights because I'd put them in my backpack," said Forge. "I groped around in the dark, and eventually managed to get off the ladder and into a horizontal crawl way. I thought I'd better move a bit further away from the sheer drop before I started messing about with my backpack, but I hit a sudden steep slope. I slid down quite a long way to somewhere flat. I've no idea where I am now, and I don't think I can get back up that slope again."

"You haven't hurt yourself, have you?" I asked anxiously.

"Only a bit."

Atticus made an exasperated noise. "What does 'only a bit' mean?"

"I cut my leg on something sharp when I slid down the slope. It's quite funny actually. I lied to Shanna about cutting my leg, and now I really *have* cut my leg."

"Yes, it's hysterically funny that the whole of Blue Zone is without power, and you're trapped in the vent system with your leg cut open," said Atticus bitterly.

"I told you I'm not seriously hurt," said Forge. "It's quite a long gash in my leg, but it seems quite shallow, and it's already stopped bleeding."

Atticus sighed. "It's a pity you didn't land on your head. There isn't much inside your skull that could be damaged."

There was an odd sound, like a metallic bing. For some reason, I looked up at the ceiling.

Atticus took his communicator from his pocket, gave the handle an extra few winds, and peered at the screen. "We've got instructions to move to the park."

CHAPTER SIXTEEN

"I'm not going to the park and leaving Forge behind," I said.

"You *are* going to the park, Amber," chorused Atticus and Forge in unison.

"You can't help Forge by hanging round our corridor, Amber," continued Atticus solo.

"I could search the area, and keep shouting into air vents until I find him."

"You can't go wandering off alone in total darkness," said Atticus. "Even if you did, you wouldn't find Forge. He's not just an unknown distance away from us horizontally, but he climbed down a ladder, so he's on Level 51 now."

"I slid down a long slope as well," said Forge. "I think I'm on Level 53, but I could even be a level or two below that. You have to forget about me, Amber, and help Atticus get the rest of our corridor group to the park."

I groaned. "All right. We'll call you again when we get to the park, Forge, and discuss how to help you. Good luck."

I ended my call, and we hurried back to where the rest of our corridor group was complaining about the taste of the ration bars and handing round a bottle of water to drink.

"We're going to move to our local park now," said Atticus.

"Why the park?" asked Shanna.

"Because that's our area evacuation centre, and it has an emergency power supply." Atticus started pulling bags out of the store room.

"Does that mean the park lights will be on?" asked Linnette hopefully.

"Yes," said Atticus. "I doubt the lights will be on at full sun brightness, they'll probably be running a version of the moons and stars programme, but they'll be on. Now everyone will have to carry their lantern, their bag, and also some of our bottles of water and ration bars."

"Why do we have to drag all those bottles of water along with us?" asked Reece. "Surely the park has an emergency water supply as well as emergency power."

"The park has a vast emergency water supply called a lake," said Atticus. "If you don't want to help carry the water bottles, Reece, then you can drink the lake water."

"We can't drink lake water," said Margot. "It's had fish and ducks swimming in it."

Atticus sighed. "The lake water would be filtered before we drank it, but if we take our bottled water with us then we can drink that first."

Ruby's voice spoke from Atticus's communicator. "Listen closely, everyone. You should have all received instructions to move to the park. We'll be using the standard convoy method, with me leading my corridor group to the north end of each of your corridors in turn so you can join us."

She paused. "My group is ready to move now. Atticus, I hope you're listening, because we'll be coming to corridor 11 first, and then moving on to corridors 13, 14 and onwards in turn."

Atticus pressed the green button. "I'm listening, Ruby."

"Good. My group is heading for corridor 11 now."

Atticus wound his communicator strap round his left wrist. "Amber, get your communicator working. You'll be leading our group, while I bring up the rear."

I wound the handle on my communicator, and checked it was working. I was already wearing my backpack. I slung a bag of ration bars over my right shoulder, picked up a bottle of water with my right hand, and my lantern with my left.

"Shouldn't the eighteen-year-olds be in charge of this?" asked Linnette.

"They should have been, but they've all gone to a Lottery candidates' event. That means it's our job to take care of the younger teens and get everyone to safety." Atticus loaded himself up with bottles and his lantern, then looked round. "Can anyone manage to carry the last bottle of water?"

"I can." Casper was already heavily loaded, but wedged the extra bottle under his right arm.

"If you start getting tired, Casper, you must ask someone else to take a turn carrying the water bottles." Atticus made a last rapid headcount, and nodded. "Amber, lead us down to the north end of the corridor."

As I headed down the corridor, I saw a gaggle of lantern lights appear at the end. When I got closer, I saw the familiar faces of the seventeen-year-olds from corridor 12. I didn't know all their names, so I wasn't sure which one was Ruby until a blonde girl sitting in a powered chair smiled at me.

"Hello, Amber," she said. "We'll move a bit further on, and then wait for you to lead your group out behind ours. This is a very wide corridor, but most of the space is taken up by the slow belt running down the middle. I don't want anyone tripping on the edge of that in the darkness, so we're moving in single file."

She waved her arm above her head in a beckoning gesture, and her powered chair started moving. A line of white lanterns followed her past the end of our corridor and then stopped. I was about to lead our group to join them, when Atticus's voice came from the communicator.

"Ruby, do you want me to bring the manual wheelchair from our emergency store room?"

"We've brought ours with us," said Ruby. "I'm hoping the charge on my powered chair will last long enough to get me to the park, but I'll have to use the manual chair after that. You might as well bring yours too. It will be useful for transporting heavy bottles of water."

Atticus groaned. "Why didn't I think of that? Wait where you are for a minute, Amber, while I get the chair." There was a clanging sound followed by a clunk. "Casper, can you load your luggage onto the chair, and push it please?"

There was a short silence before Atticus spoke again. "Sorry for the delay, Ruby. We're ready to go now. Lead us out to join the others, Amber."

As I started moving, I was startled to hear the sound of a hunting horn from behind me. I turned to see what was going on, and a figure seemed to leap out from nowhere. It was swathed in a black cloak and wearing the red-eyed helm of the hunter of souls.

CHAPTER SEVENTEEN

The others all screamed at the sight of the nightmare figure, dropped their bags and bottles, and turned to flee back down our corridor. I would have started running myself, but it was less than two days since I'd been terrified by Forge appearing out of a hole in my room wall, and only hours since I'd spoken to an actor playing the role of the hunter of souls.

I couldn't believe that a creature out of the Halloween myths had really appeared in our corridor. It seemed far more likely that this was one of our corridor group wearing an old Halloween costume, and I didn't need to try to remember who had dressed as the hunter of souls last Halloween. There was only one of us stupid enough, and cruel enough, to play an evil trick like this.

"It's only Reece!" I yelled.

Margot had tripped over a bag of emergency ration bars, and gone sprawling on the corridor floor. The hunter of souls was standing over her, flapping his black cloak at her, and laughing at her desperate attempts to crawl away from him. I used the bottle of water I was carrying in my right hand as a weapon, sweeping it into his legs with all my strength, so he toppled over onto the floor.

"It's only Reece," I yelled again. "He's wearing his costume from last Halloween."

People had scattered down the length of the corridor, most of them still clutching their lanterns. The nearer ones heard me, and turned to look back. Reece was trying to get up again, so I dumped my lantern on the floor, and jumped on top of him.

Reece threw me off him, sending me flying against the wall, but I'd managed to pull off his red-eyed helm. The others could see his face in the light of my lantern now, and Margot and Atticus led a rush of people to help me. Margot grabbed Reece's hair, and began beating his head against the floor, so I had to swap from fighting Reece to preventing Margot from killing him. Atticus's face was flushed with embarrassment and fury as he shouted out in a breathless voice.

"I'm putting Reece under arrest until we can hand him over to the hasties. I'll need some rope or tape to tie him up."

"Hand me over to the hasties?" Reece was looking scared now. "You can't do that. You're overreacting to a harmless joke."

"Harmless joke?" repeated Atticus savagely. "There was nothing harmless or funny about what you did. You terrified everyone, and threw someone who's recovering from a head injury against a wall."

Atticus turned to look anxiously at me. "How is your head, Amber?"

I'd been so angry with Reece, that I'd totally forgotten I needed to be careful not to bump my head. I lifted a hand to check the lump of glue in my hair. "I think I'm all right."

I'd heard Ruby's voice coming from my communicator during the fight. She spoke again now. "What's going on back there? What was all the screaming about?"

Atticus yanked his communicator out of his pocket and spoke into it. "When I was getting the manual wheelchair, Reece decided it would be really funny to sneak off to his room, put on his old Halloween costume, and jump out at people pretending he was the hunter of souls. My corridor group scattered down the corridor, dropping things as they ran. I just hope none of the lanterns have broken."

"Waste that!" said Ruby. "We'll come back and take charge of Reece for you, while you collect your people together."

Preeja came running up with a roll of tape. Atticus knelt beside Reece and taped his wrists together.

"I won't be able to walk to the park with my wrists taped together," protested Reece.

"I'm not sure we'll bother taking you to the park," said Atticus savagely. "After all the trouble you've caused, I may just lock you in the emergency store room for the hasties to collect later."

"You were all mean to me, sending a telepath squad after me and dumping me for Carnival," said Reece. "You can't blame me for wanting to get a little of my own back."

"Oh yes, I can blame you," said Atticus. "I can blame you a lot."

"I can blame you too." Shanna offered Atticus a length of cloth. "I think you should gag Reece with this."

"Good idea." Atticus tied the cloth round Reece's mouth, and then stood up. "Roll call, everyone."

As Atticus started calling names, I noticed Margot sidle up to where Reece was lying on the floor, and give him a furtive kick in the ribs. I couldn't blame her for that, but was thinking I'd have to intervene if she did it again, when I was distracted by Atticus repeating a name.

"Linnette? Can anyone see Linnette?"

No one answered.

Atticus frowned, called the last three names and got answers, then tried shouting for Linnette again without success. "Did anyone see what happened to Linnette in the panic?"

"Linnette and I were together when Reece jumped out at us," said Margot. "We turned round and started running back down our corridor. I know Linnette was just ahead of me when she dropped her bag of ration bars, because I tripped over it and fell. Reece leaned over me then, flapping his cloak to frighten me, so I didn't see what happened to Linnette after that."

"Did anyone else see Linnette?" asked Atticus.

"I only remember seeing Reece and Margot," I said.

Atticus stooped over Reece, and pulled down his gag. "Did you see what happened to Linnette?"

"The coward ran into her room," said Reece sulkily. "She's probably still hiding in there."

"I'll get her." Margot hurried down the corridor and started calling through Linnette's door.

As Atticus gagged Reece again, Ruby came bowling up in her powered chair, with two muscled boys chasing after her. The boys grabbed Reece by the arms, and Ruby looked round at where people were collecting bottles and bags.

"How much damage is there?" she asked.

"It looks like the lanterns all survived, and only one of the water bottles split," said Atticus. "I'm planning to deal with that by making Reece drink lake water. We just need to coax Linnette out of her room and we can start moving."

Ruby spoke into her communicator. "Corridor 13, we'll be coming to you next. I hope you aren't having any problems with troublemakers playing tricks."

"I had one person starting to tell Halloween stories," said a grim female voice, "but I locked her in our emergency store room for fifteen minutes. She's behaving herself now."

Margot came back to join us. "I called through Linnette's door, and told her that it wasn't the hunter of souls attacking us, only Reece being horrible as usual. I said it was safe to come out of her room again, and I heard her sob a couple of times, but she won't open the door. I tried calling her dataview, but she's not answering that either."

"Does anyone know the code for Linnette's door?" asked Atticus.

There was silence.

He groaned. "You need special equipment to override a room door lock, and Emergency Services will be too busy with high priority lift rescues to send anyone to help."

"I'd better carry on and collect the other corridor groups while you persuade Linnette out of her room," said Ruby. "I can bring the convoy back for your group at the end."

"You need to get everyone to the park, not take them walking in circles round dark corridors," said Atticus. "Amber can take the rest of our corridor group with you now, while I stay here with Linnette. If I can coax her into moving, then we'll follow you to the park later, otherwise we'll wait things out here until the power is on."

Atticus was keeping his face and voice calm and controlled.

The strained expression in his eyes, and the slight tremble of the hand holding his lantern, betrayed the truth though. He was forcing himself to do what he believed was his duty, but he was scared of the dark and getting dangerously close to breaking point.

I remembered climbing the cliff on Teen Level beach. I'd been coping until I looked down, but then my fear of heights overwhelmed me. If Atticus stayed here with Linnette, then an unexpected flicker from his lantern, or a disturbing shadow, could mean that his fear of the dark overwhelmed him in exactly the same way.

I couldn't let that happen. "You're right that one of us needs to take the rest of our group to the park, while the other stays here with Linnette, but it should be me that stays rather than you."

"I have to be the one to stay," said Atticus. "What happened was totally my fault. I should have tied up Reece the first time he started causing trouble, but I'm used to trailing round after Forge rather than making decisions myself."

I felt a huge wave of sympathy for Atticus. He trailed round after Forge. I trailed round after Shanna. Given the choice, neither of us would have been taking a leadership role in this situation.

"What happened was Reece's fault, not yours," I said. "It's much more sensible for me to stay here. I'll be better at reassuring Linnette."

Ruby shook her head. "You can't stay here, Amber. You haven't had warden training."

I shrugged. "I don't see that I need warden training to sit outside Linnette's door and talk to her. If I have any problems, I can use my communicator to call you, and you can give me advice."

"I suppose that's true," said Ruby doubtfully.

"The crucial point right now is that the rest of you are scared of the dark but I'm not," I said. "The Halloween stories about the hunter of souls and the darkness have never worried me. I'm frightened by stories about the daylight Outside, and how the Truesun can blind you, but that's hardly likely to matter."

Ruby nodded. "All right. Amber stays."

Atticus's expression was an odd mixture of frustration and relief. "You've got your own lantern, Amber. If my counting is right then Linnette has a lantern in her room with her. We'll leave you Reece's lantern as well, and plenty of water and ration bars."

Ruby and the boys went back to their own corridor group after that, taking Reece with them. Atticus got our group organized again and started them moving. I followed them down to the north end of the corridor, and watched the lanterns of my friends join those of Ruby's group. As they moved off, Atticus turned back for a moment to wave at me, and then he followed them. A minute later, my lantern was the only light in the darkness.

I had a ridiculous moment of panic. It wasn't the darkness that was bothering me, but the fact I was alone. I'd been living on Teen Level since I was thirteen. I was used to its corridors being crammed with other teens. Now all the teens in the area were moving to the park and leaving me behind. I felt abandoned and isolated.

I reminded myself that I hadn't been abandoned. I'd volunteered to do this, and I could use my communicator to talk to Atticus and Ruby if I needed help. I wasn't alone either. Linnette was here, locked in her room, and I should focus on helping her.

I went back to Linnette's door, with its stack of supplies next to it. I wound up both my own lantern and the spare one, then tried calling through the door.

"It's me, Amber. I'm sitting outside your door with two lanterns. Why don't you let me in to join you? Think how bright your room would be with three lanterns in there."

I waited a minute but there was no reply. I tried again. "If you're getting thirsty or hungry, then I've got water bottles and ration bars."

Linnette didn't say anything, she was probably too frozen in terror to speak, but I heard a faint, high-pitched, hiccupping sob.

"Well, I'm right here," I said. "When you're feeling a bit better, you can open the door and let me in, or just try talking to me."

I was suffering that horrible feeling of isolation again. I took out my communicator, turned it on, and comforted myself by listening to Ruby and the other wardens talking. Once all the corridor groups had joined the convoy, they started heading for our local park.

There was a babble of conversation on the way to the park, a rush of rejoicing voices when the convoy arrived, and then the communicator abruptly went silent. Everyone was in the familiar territory of our local park, with proper lights again, so they wouldn't need the communicators.

I sat in the pool of light cast by my two lanterns. The total silence was unnerving. Wherever you were in the Hive, whatever the hour of the day or night, there'd always be the reassuring background hum of air vents and lights. On Teen Level, there was usually the sound of distant voices or laughter as well. Now there was nothing at all.

I was tempted to use my dataview to play music, but it would be foolish to drain its power when I could be stuck here for days. The light of my lanterns started wavering, so I wound them up again. Linnette should surely have calmed down a little by now, so I tried calling through the door again.

"I'm still out here, Linnette. Please talk to me."

There was no answer. I pictured Linnette huddled in her room, and tried to think what I could say to reach through the fog of terror in her mind. I remembered how Buzz had used the tactic of chatting about her own experiences to encourage me to relax and talk to her.

"I understand you being scared of Halloween stories and the dark," I said. "I'm just as terrified of heights. Remember our beach trip, and how I panicked on the cliff climb? I was fine until I looked down, but then the ground seemed a thousand levels below me, and I started shaking with fear."

I sighed. "I should have climbed down right away, but instead I did the ridiculous thing of climbing with my eyes closed. That was how I managed to hit my head on the ceiling. It was horribly embarrassing when I was at the medical facility, having to explain to the doctor that I'd hit my head on a star."

I felt I was bound to hear a comment or at least a noise from Linnette. I waited, but there was nothing.

I frowned and continued. "Have I ever told you why I'm scared of heights? It started when I was seven years old. I'd climbed a tree in our local park, and was trying to write my name on the ceiling, when a branch broke under my weight. I fell out of the tree and broke my arm."

There was no response from inside the door. Not even another sob. I was getting seriously worried now. Was Linnette all right in there? Had she somehow had an accident? I pictured her lying unconscious on the floor of her room.

I abandoned the subtle approach, and tried yelling and banging on the door. "Linnette. Say something, or at least make a noise. I need to know that you're all right."

There still wasn't the faintest sound from the other side of the door.

"Waste this!" I glared at Linnette's door, and remembered how Reece had managed to get into my room because I'd chosen such an obvious door code.

I started punching in some simple door codes, beginning with my own old door code, 54321, then 12345, and moving on to 11111, 22222, and working my way upwards. When I got to 55555, there was a click from the door, and it drifted open a fraction.

I stared at it in stunned disbelief for a couple of seconds, then grabbed both my lanterns, and elbowed the door wide open. "Linnette, are you...?" I let the words trail off, because the room was empty.

CHAPTER EIGHTEEN

I checked the shower and every storage space in Linnette's room, even those that were too small to hide a rabbit. She definitely wasn't in there, and that didn't make any sense. Reece had said that Linnette had locked herself in this room, Margot had said she'd heard a sobbing sound through the door, and I'd heard what I thought was a sob myself.

Linnette couldn't have sneaked out of the room without me seeing her. She couldn't have gone exploring in the air vent system, because there wasn't an inspection hatch in this room. She couldn't have vanished into thin air. That meant she hadn't locked herself in here at all when Reece scared her, just gone running off into the darkness.

I could believe Reece had lied about that, afraid how the rest of us would react if he admitted the truth. I was wondering what had made the sobbing noise that had fooled me and Margot, when I heard it again, coming from the shower.

I went to investigate, and found the shower had been left turned on. Presumably Linnette had either been about to have a shower, or had just finished having one, when the power went off. The shower had stopped working, but the occasional drip of water was still falling from it, making a soft, vaguely musical note when it landed on the floor.

I turned off the shower, took out my dataview, and tried calling Linnette. There was no answer. I tried calling her twice more, and then took out my communicator.

"Ruby? Atticus? Is one of you there?"

"I'm here," said Ruby's voice.

"Me too," said Atticus. "Have you got Linnette out of her room yet?"

"I'm afraid I've got bad news about that. I managed to guess Linnette's door code, and got into her room, but she wasn't there."

"You mean Reece deliberately lied about her going in there!" Atticus sounded as if he was about to explode with anger.

"Yes. Linnette must have run off in terror. I've tried calling her dataview, but she doesn't answer. She must be lost or injured somewhere, so I'm going to look for her."

"You can't do that, Amber," said Ruby sharply. "You'll get lost yourself."

"No, I won't. I've got two lanterns with me, so I'll have plenty of light, and I'll be careful to stay in the area I know well."

"We can't have any more people getting lost," said Ruby. "I'm your emergency group leader, Amber. I'm ordering you to come to the park, and you have to obey me."

I was a dutiful member of the Hive. As a small child, I'd broken a few rules out of ignorance. As a teen, I'd indulged in a few of the accepted minor transgressions, such as riding the handrail. I'd never had more than a scolding from a bored hasty, never had a bad report on my record, and certainly never dreamed of disobeying a direct order from someone in authority.

Ruby might only be another teen like me, but she was acting emergency group leader, and that put her in a position of authority. I should obey her and go to the park. I wanted to obey her, because I was feeling horribly alone here. I wasn't going to do it though. Linnette was lost somewhere in a maze of pitch black corridors, Forge was trapped in the vent system, and I was the only person in a position to help either of them.

I'd openly defy Ruby if I had to, but it was worth trying persuasion first. "It makes sense for me to at least search for Linnette on my way to the park. I can go to the south end of our corridor, and take the route past the accommodation corridors and through the shopping area to reach one of the park side entrances."

"There's a shorter route from the north end of our corridor to the main park entrance," said Atticus.

"Yes, but we know Linnette didn't go that way. When Reece jumped out and scared us all, we were down the north end of the corridor. Everyone turned and ran south until I called to them to stop. Linnette must have failed to hear me, or been too terrified to listen, and kept running south."

"All right," said Ruby. "I'll agree to you taking the longer route to get to the park, Amber, but you mustn't go wandering off anywhere else."

I made a vague noise that could be interpreted as acceptance, put the communicator back in my pocket, and considered the issue of what to take with me and how best to carry it. I managed to wedge a water bottle and a dozen ration bars into my bag, and slung that on my back. One of the lanterns was starting to flicker, so I wound them both, picked up one in each hand, and headed to the south end of the corridor before stopping.

I needed to turn east to reach the shopping area, but Linnette could have gone west. It was possible that she hadn't gone far, and was huddled somewhere close by, too terrified to move. I tried calling her name first, then turned off my lanterns and stood in total darkness, looking for any distant glimmer of light.

I couldn't see anything at all. I turned my lanterns on again, called Linnette's name one last time, and then turned to walk east. When I reached the end of corridor 12, I paused to do the same routine as before, and then repeated it again at the end of each of the other corridors.

At the end of corridor 15, I saw something lying on the ground. I pounced on it eagerly, thinking Linnette might have dropped it, but then I saw it was a fluffy, white toy rabbit, the sort of thing that would belong to a very young child.

I picked it up and studied it in bewilderment, wondering what it was doing here on Teen Level. Corridor 15 held fourteen-year-olds. It was just under a year since their families, all dressed in basic clothes to hide their level, had been carrying bags and belongings to these rooms and saying farewell. Was the rabbit a treasured parting gift from a small brother or sister? When I arrived on Teen Level myself, eight-year-old Gregas had only been interested in arguing his case for taking over my old bedroom, but I could imagine other brothers and sisters being more affectionate.

I put the rabbit over by the wall, where its owner would hopefully find it later, and moved on. There were neatly stacked piles of boxes by the wall between the end of corridor 19 and the end of corridor 20. Those would be for the eighteen-year-olds to pack their possessions before they left for Lottery. A year from now, I'd be packing my things myself, and heading off into an unknown future. The thought gave me a nervous churning in my stomach, but I couldn't let myself be distracted by thoughts of Lottery now.

I must have walked this route to the shopping area at least a hundred times during my years on Teen Level, but everything looked confusingly different with the lantern light casting huge, distorted shadows. I reached a crossroads, where I could turn right for a belt system interchange, or left for the laundry. I needed to go straight on.

I was passing narrow corridors on either side of me now. Those were all accommodation corridors; 21 to 30 on the left, and 31 to 40 on the right. I paused at the end of each corridor to look for lights and shout Linnette's name, but without success.

As I neared the junction with accommodation corridor 30 on one side and 40 on the other, I saw something odd ahead of me. Right at the edge of my lantern light, something too solid to be just shadows was sprawling across my path. I advanced cautiously, and finally worked out that a mass of boxes were strewn across the corridor.

I'd already passed one neatly stacked mountain of boxes. There must have been a similar mountain here too, but someone had collided with it and sent the boxes tumbling across the corridor floor. Had that person been Linnette, running in blind panic from the hunter of souls?

I advanced on the boxes, saw one had been crushed and showed the distinct outline of a foot, while several others had been flattened in a way that suggested someone had fallen on them. There was a glint as something reflected the light of my lanterns. I bent down to pick it up. It was a dataview, with a familiar decoration of bright blue and mauve flowers. It belonged to Linnette.

CHAPTER NINETEEN

This explained why Linnette hadn't answered any of our calls. She'd collided with these boxes, fallen, and lost her dataview. Since she wasn't here, she must have picked herself up and started running again, but had she gone straight on or turned down one of the corridors on either side?

"Linnette!" I called at the top of my voice. "Linnette, are you there? It's me, Amber."

I turned off my lanterns, but there was only unbroken blackness around me, so I turned them back on again. I walked the length of corridor 30 and back, but there was no hint that Linnette had turned to run down there, no sign of disorder at all. This corridor would hold eighteen-year-olds, and they were probably all at the same event as the eighteen-year-olds in my own corridor group.

I checked corridor 40 as well, and couldn't see anything unusual, except that each door had been decorated with a picture. They were all cartoon birds or animals with a hint of human features. I guessed that a budding artist lived on this corridor and had done these pictures of his or her friends.

Linnette must have run straight on down the main corridor. I moved on myself and reached a crossroads. Turning right or going straight on would take me to more blocks of accommodation corridors. Turning left would take me to the shopping area. I'd walked this way so many times that turning left here was an ingrained habit. Had that same ingrained habit made Linnette turn left as well, or had fear triumphed, sending her running straight on?

"Linnette!" I yelled.

I thought I heard an answer, and called again several times, before working out that it was only some oddity of the area sending an echo of my own voice back to me. I hesitated, and then turned left, walking down a short, blank-walled corridor that made one abrupt, ninety-degree turn before reaching the shopping area.

I was used to this place being filled with the bright lights of competing shop displays. Now it was just a massive black void. I walked straight forward for a minute, then paused to call for Linnette and look round for other lantern lights. I was about to move on, when I realized I wasn't sure which way I was facing any longer. The pool of light around me didn't reach far enough for me to see any walls or shops. There was a bench to one side of me, and a structural pillar ahead, but I knew there were a dozen benches and any number of pillars in the shopping area.

I frowned, walked in what I thought was a forward direction, and found the unmistakable landmark of the upway and downway. The moving stairs were frozen in place, the steps of the downway seeming far steeper than usual, leading down into utter blackness.

I knew the moving stairs were in the middle of the shopping area. I called Linnette's name a couple of times, but most of my mind was occupied with working out which way I was facing. I was about to walk on, when I heard a faint sound.

Was that another echo or a real person? I tried calling again. "Linnette, it's me, Amber!"

I heard the sound again. I thought it was a human voice, but it was very quiet and distorted, so I couldn't make out any words. One thing was obvious though, the sound was coming from the menacing black depths of the downway.

I groaned, cowardly bought myself a minute of respite by winding up both lanterns, and then forced myself to walk across to the steps and call out. "Linnette!"

There was an answering cry that could have been saying the

word help. Either Linnette or someone else was definitely down there. I moistened my lips, and reminded myself how many times I'd ridden on the moving stairs. These frozen steps would be steep, but nothing like the sheer drop of a lift shaft. I'd be in no danger if I moved slowly and carefully.

"Linnette, I'm coming!"

I descended cautiously, taking one step at a time, and found Linnette lying in a crumpled heap. I put my lanterns down, and knelt anxiously beside her. "Linnette, where are you hurt?"

Her eyes were closed and she didn't respond.

"Linnette!" I called in panic.

There was still no response. I touched her neck, and felt the reassuring beat of her pulse. I was wondering what to do, trying to remember what I'd been taught in the first aid activity sessions, when Linnette's eyes flickered open. She gave me a confused look, and then moaned in pain.

"Where are you hurt?" I asked urgently. "Did you hit your head?"

"No, it's my leg that hurts. How did you find me, Amber?"

"First I found your dataview, and then I heard you shouting for help." I tucked Linnette's dataview in her pocket.

"Did I shout for help?" She sounded puzzled. "I remember the hunter of souls attacking us. Everyone was screaming and running." Her voice abruptly rose in fear. "The hunter of souls hasn't followed us here, has he?"

"No, he isn't here. It wasn't the real hunter of souls anyway, just Reece dressed in his old Halloween outfit."

"Reece." Linnette was silent for a moment, as if trying to absorb that. "It can't have been Reece. The hunter of souls was chasing me, and then I ran straight into his demon pack. They all leapt out to attack me."

"I think you bumped into a stack of boxes, and they fell on you," I broke the news as gently as I could. "I can understand you assuming it was the demon pack attacking you, but there was only ever Reece playing a horribly cruel trick. I hope he gets into serious trouble for it."

"You're sure it was just boxes?" Linnette didn't wait for me to reply. "I thought I saw eyes and teeth, so I kept running and didn't look back. I didn't know where I was until I saw the downway ahead of me in the lantern light. I tried to stop, but I was going too fast and fell. I grabbed at the handrail, but missed it, and then there was a dreadful pain in my leg."

She paused. "The only thing I can remember after that is the sound of my lantern going clattering down the stairs. I think I must have fainted."

"You hurt your leg when you fell? Which one?"

"My left leg. It's still hurting a lot. I must have pulled a muscle or..." Linnette tried to sit up, gave a strangled gasp of pain, and then slumped backwards.

Linnette's eyes were closed again. She seemed to have fainted from the pain. I peered down at her left leg. Even in the limited light of the lanterns, I could see there was something unnatural about the shape of it.

I took my dataview from my pocket, and was about to call Emergency Services for help, when there was the chiming sound of an incoming call. I automatically answered it.

"I heard shouting a few minutes ago," said Forge. "Was that you, Amber? It sounded like your voice, so I tried shouting back."

"Yes, that was me shouting." I was overwhelmed with relief that Forge had escaped from the vent system. "I heard someone answering me, but the voice was so distorted I didn't realize it was you. I'm with Linnette. We're on the downway between Teen Level 50 and Level 51. Linnette's fallen and hurt herself, so I need you to come and help us."

"I'm afraid I can't come anywhere," said Forge. "I'm still stuck in the vent system."

"Oh. I assumed you'd somehow got out and..." I groaned my disappointment. I'd thought Forge was safe, and that he'd take over the responsibility for Linnette, but neither of those things were true.

"I think I'm on Level 53 or 54," said Forge. "I'm next to an inspection hatch, and heard your voice in the distance."

"You must be in an air vent next to the downway, and it's somehow carrying the sound up to me. That explains why your voice was so muffled and distorted."

"Yes," said Forge. "That steep slope I slipped down must have been where the air vent sloped down beside the downway, but what are you and Linnette doing on the downway? Everyone should be in the park by now."

"Reece jumped out and scared everyone. Linnette went running off into the darkness. I went to look for her, and found she'd fallen on the downway. I think she's broken her leg."

"When I get out of here, I'll make sure Health and Safety deal with Reece." Forge's voice held a savagely angry note. "You need to call Emergency Services for help right away."

"Yes. When they've helped Linnette, I may be able to get them to rescue you as well."

"Forget about me," said Forge. "All that matters is getting help for Linnette. Call Emergency Services now."

Forge ended his call, and I tapped at my dataview.

"This is Emergency Services," said a female voice.

"I need urgent medical help for…"

I let my sentence trail off because the voice was still speaking, obviously a recording rather than a real person.

"Blue Zone is currently experiencing a widespread emergency. If there is an emergency warden in your area, you should end this call and report your problem to them for assessment and appropriate escalation. If there is no emergency warden available, please give your name and identity code."

"Amber 2514-0172-912."

"Do you have a lift emergency, medical emergency, fire emergency, or other emergency?" asked the recorded voice.

"Medical emergency."

"What is your exact location including both area and level?"

"I'm in area 510/6120, on the downway between the shopping areas on Teen Level 50 and Level 51. Please come quickly."

The recorded voice continued with its relentless questioning. "Please give a short description of your medical emergency."

I groaned. "Linnette fell down the stairs. She broke her left leg and fainted." I peered at Linnette's face, and saw her eyes were still closed. "She was talking to me a couple of minutes ago, but she's fainted again."

There was a pause of a few seconds before the voice spoke again. "Are there any hazards in your location that could endanger a rescue team?"

"It's very dark," I said, with an edge of sarcasm. "They should take care not to fall on the downway."

Another pause. "This call will now be ended to free the connection for other emergency calls. Medical Emergency Triage will call you as soon as possible."

My dataview flashed a call ended message at me.

CHAPTER TWENTY

What? Emergency Services had ended my call! I glared at my dataview in outrage. Yes, I could reluctantly accept the point about freeing the connection for other emergency callers, but it wasn't very helpful to tell me Medical Emergency Triage would call me as soon as possible. That could mean anything from ten minutes to ten hours. What was I supposed to do while I was waiting for...?

My dataview chimed, I tapped it to answer the call, and a man's voice spoke. "This is Medical Emergency Triage. Amber, you reported an injured person with a broken leg."

"Yes," I said eagerly.

"I need to check the details with you. Is it correct that the injured person is named Linnette, and currently in area 510/6120, on the downway between the shopping areas on Teen Level 50 and Level 51?"

"That's right."

"Do you have any further identity information for the injured person?"

"She's Linnette 2514-1003-947."

"Area 510/6120, corridor 11, room 18?"

"Yes, that's her."

"Thank you. Casualty identity confirmed. Is Linnette conscious at the moment?"

I glanced at Linnette, saw her eyes were open again now, and she was staring at the lanterns.

"Yes."

"Does she have a head injury?"

"No."

"Wait one moment please."

I waited impatiently. It was at least five minutes before the man's voice spoke again.

"Unfortunately, we do not have a rescue team in your vicinity, Amber. With the lifts and belt system out of operation, our rescue teams have to travel to locations and take casualties for treatment on foot. This means response times are far slower than usual. Our nearest teams already have a heavy queue of serious, closer calls to answer, so their current estimated response time is not a viable option for you."

"Not a viable option? But..."

The man kept talking. "Your local medical facility has evacuated to your area park. I've tried contacting them and asking if they can despatch assistance to you, but they are overloaded with new casualties in need of urgent treatment. You'll have to take Linnette to the park for treatment yourself."

"What? Me? How?"

"I need you to listen closely to my instructions, Amber," said the man, in soothing tones. "There is an emergency store room on the north side of every shopping area. The door is marked with a red cross. The door code is 999, followed by the area code, followed by the level. You need to get a wheeled stretcher, a pack of strength three pain relief medication, and a box marked adult leg protection. Have you done the basic first aid activities on Teen Level?"

I was too busy panicking to reply.

"Amber? Have you done the basic first aid activities on Teen Level?"

"Yes."

"Good. The pack of strength three pain medication will contain two tablets. You should give both tablets to Linnette, then wrap the protection unit around her leg and inflate it. After that, you move her onto the stretcher to take her to the park. On arrival, you must hand the empty pain medication pack to the medical staff so they know exactly what tablets Linnette has been given. Do you understand?"

"Yes, but the stretcher won't work on the stairs of the downway."

"You'll have to move Linnette up the steps."

I gnawed at my bottom lip. "Won't that hurt her leg?"

"The inflated protection unit should prevent any further damage. I have to deal with other calls now, Amber. If you discover Linnette has any additional injuries, you should call Emergency Services again for more instructions."

The call ended. I tucked my dataview into my pocket, and ran my fingers through my hair. I shouldn't be doing this. Linnette needed help from experts, not from someone who'd attended two first aid sessions over a year ago.

There was a whimper from Linnette. "The lights are flickering."

"Yes, sorry." There weren't any experts to help Linnette, there was only me, so I had to stop panicking and do the best I could. I wound both the lanterns, and tried to speak in a calm, confident voice.

"Emergency Services have told me to fetch some painkillers and other things for you. I'll only be going as far as the shopping area emergency store room. I'll need to take one lantern with me, but the other will stay here with you, and I promise I'll be back in a few minutes. Is that all right?"

"Painkillers," Linnette breathed the word in a voice of desperate hope. "Yes."

I picked up one of the lanterns, and moved carefully up the stairs to the Level 50 shopping area. Once I reached its black void, I paused to try to picture the layout, and headed in the direction I thought was north.

A minute later, I was standing by a clothes shop that was definitely on the east side of the shopping area. I worked my way along the line of shops until I reached the north side, and eventually tracked down the emergency store room.

I'd been worried I'd forget the door code, but that wasn't a problem. The door was already wide open, and several empty boxes told me that someone, probably several people, had already been here for medical supplies. I should have expected that. The shopping area would have been crowded when the lights went out and the moving stairs suddenly jerked to a halt. There would obviously have been injuries.

I held up my lantern and peered anxiously inside the room. Every shelf and space was neatly labelled with what its contents should be. The two wheelchairs had gone, but the wheeled stretcher was still in place. The limb protection boxes were in a jumble where someone had sorted through them in a hurry. There must have been several casualties with arm or wrist injuries, because the arm protection unit boxes were all empty. I thought the leg protection units were gone too, but found one had tumbled on the floor.

The medication shelf was half empty. I hunted through the remaining small packets, and was relieved to find one labelled strength three pain relief. I tucked that in my pocket, and unfolded the stretcher. I was expecting to struggle to find my way back to Linnette, but I could see a very faint glow in the darkness that had to be coming from the lantern I'd left with her. I towed the stretcher across to the top of the downway, and left it there while I went down the steps to Linnette.

"I'm sorry that took longer than I expected," I said.

She made a dismissive gesture with her left hand. "Do you have the painkillers?"

"Yes." I put my lantern and the leg protection unit box down on the stairs, and took out the packet. "Is your leg still hurting you?"

"Of course it's still hurting me," Linnette snapped, in a terse, angry voice that I'd never heard her use before.

I hastily got the two tablets out of the packet, gave them to Linnette, and held the water bottle to her lips so she could gulp down some water. I waited a couple of minutes, and then wrapped the leg protection unit round her leg and inflated it.

"Is that better?"

"That's so much better." Linnette gave a soft sigh of relief and leant back on the stairs.

Now I had to get Linnette off the steps so I could use the stretcher. It would be easier for us to go down the stairs, but I could barely find my way around the Level 50 shopping area that I knew very well. I'd get hopelessly lost on Level 51, and I had no idea where their park was anyway, so we should try to go up instead.

"Linnette, we need to get you to the stretcher so I can take you to the park. If you sit up, then I'll get behind you and pull."

There was no answer. I saw her eyes were closed.

"Linnette?" I gave her arm a shake, but she just made a murmuring noise in response, and I realized that she was fast asleep. My painkilling tablets had had a similar effect on me but it hadn't happened this quickly. At least this meant Linnette wouldn't be in pain when I moved her.

I positioned myself behind Linnette, put my arms round her, and pulled, but she was heavier than I expected and didn't move. I braced myself, tried pulling again, and managed to lift her a fraction but not enough to get her up to the next step.

I gave a groan of utter despair. I wasn't strong enough to haul Linnette up the stairs. If I went below her and pulled, then I might be able to drag her down the stairs feet first, but that could injure her broken leg. On the other hand, turning her round, and pulling her down the stairs head first, would be even more dangerous.

I tried to think things through calmly and logically. If I called Ruby or Atticus, and explained the situation, then I was sure Atticus would attempt to reach me despite his fear of the dark. That would take a long time though, and there was a risk he'd get lost or hurt on the way.

Forge had said he was next to an inspection hatch. If I could find him, and get that inspection hatch open, then he could help me with Linnette. I took out my dataview and tapped at it.

"Forge, I need you to start calling out to me, so I can follow the sound of your voice and get you out of that air vent."

"I told you to forget about me and concentrate on helping Linnette."

"Linnette is the reason I need to get you out of that air vent. Emergency Services can't get a rescue team to us, so I have to get Linnette to the park myself. I've got a wheeled stretcher, but Linnette's lying on the downway. I'm not strong enough to carry her up the stairs to the stretcher, but you are."

CHAPTER TWENTY-ONE

Linnette was safe in the depths of sleep, free from pain and fear, but I left my backpack, the water bottle, and one of the lanterns with her in case she woke up. I picked up the other lantern in my right hand, and moved cautiously down the stairs.

When I reached Level 51, the downway flattened out and turned sharply, before turning into steps again and heading down to Level 52. I paused on the flat section to listen to the muffled shouts from Forge. They were still distant enough that I guessed he was at least two levels down from me.

I started moving again, my attention still on Forge's voice, so I didn't see the object on the ground until I stepped on it. The thing rolled under my right foot, tipping me backwards. Arms flailing desperately, I dropped my lantern as I tried to grab the handrails, missed both of them, and fell heavily.

I landed on my back, shocked, and sickeningly aware of an agonizing pain in my right ankle. Waste it! I'd fallen and hurt my leg, just as Linnette had done. If I'd broken my ankle, then I was in deep trouble. Even worse than that, if I'd broken my ankle then Linnette and Forge were in deep trouble too.

My ankle was throbbing so badly that I didn't dare to try to get up. I lay perfectly still, hoping the pain would soon ease, and gazed longingly at the glow of my lantern. It had hit the ground hard, bounced a couple of times, and landed well out of my reach, but it was still bravely shining as a beacon in the darkness.

My lantern had survived my fall without suffering any

serious damage. I just had to hope my ankle had been as lucky. I could hear Forge calling my name at intervals, but I didn't try to reply. There was no point in worrying him with the news that I'd had an accident until I knew whether I'd injured myself or not.

One minute went by, two minutes, and I could convince myself that the pain in my ankle had eased. After another minute, I was sure of it. Once the pain was down to a dull ache, I warily tried to get up. Yes, my right ankle could take my weight without any new stabs of pain. It wasn't broken, just bruised and sore.

I stood there, gripping the handrail tightly for a moment longer, while my shaken nerves relaxed. I'd been lucky, incredibly lucky to survive my fall without serious damage to myself or my lantern. I had to make sure that I didn't have any more accidents, because I couldn't depend on being that lucky again.

I wanted to go over to retrieve my lantern, but I'd stepped on something once and fallen, and mustn't do it again. I knelt down, and groped around for the mysterious object. When I had it in my hands, I realized it wasn't mysterious at all. Linnette had come running through the shopping area, seen the downway too late to stop, and fallen halfway down the flight of stairs. She'd lost her grip on her lantern, and it had fallen all the way to the bottom.

I made the hopelessly optimistic gesture of winding Linnette's lantern, and was stunned when it flared into life. It made sense that emergency lanterns were designed to be tough enough to survive minor falls, but I felt this one was truly heroic to have crashed the length of the downway and still function.

Forge was still calling my name at intervals. The shouts were getting more frequent, and I could hear an anxious note in his voice. He was obviously worried after hearing absolutely nothing from me for several minutes.

"I'm getting closer! Keep shouting," I yelled.

I collected and wound both the lanterns, and headed on down to Level 52, moving with paranoid care. This time I had the sense to stand still while I listened to Forge's voice and tried to gauge his position. He was definitely a lot closer now, probably on Level 53.

I moved on, with Forge's voice getting gradually louder. When I reached Level 53, he sounded very close, though still a little below me. As I turned the corner, and began moving down the next flight of stairs, I heard him give a cry of excitement.

"Amber, I can see your light!"

I stopped, looked upwards, and saw an inspection hatch in the wall to my left. There was a glint of light from behind it, which had to be the lights attached to Forge's silly headband.

"I can see your lights too," I called back.

I'd found Forge, but I had a new problem now. That inspection hatch was much too high up for me to reach it. If I searched the shops in the Level 53 shopping area, would I be able to find a ladder? Even if I did, how could I position a ladder safely on the treacherous, frozen steps of the downway?

One handrail of the downway ran close to the wall with the inspection hatch. If I stood on it, would that be enough to give me the extra height that I needed?

The only way to find out was to try standing on the handrail. I stood next to it, positioned ready to jump up, but hesitated. I was used to illegally riding the handrail, balancing precariously on it as it dived down the levels of the Hive, but I'd always done it under glaringly bright lights. Now there was just the light of my lantern, the handrail looked as if it was plunging down into a bottomless, black pit.

"I can't see anything through the grille on this inspection hatch except light and shadows," said Forge. "Are you below me now?"

"Yes." I wound up the lanterns and put them down on the stairs on either side of me.

"How far below me?"

I didn't answer. I was busy telling myself that I could do this. I'd often ridden the handrail for as long as ten or fifteen levels before being sternly ordered off by the hasties. This time, I'd only need to balance on it for a minute, two at most, while I unclipped that inspection hatch.

"How far below me?" repeated Forge.

"Far enough below you that I'll have to stand on the handrail of the downway to reach the hatch."

"Watch out when you undo the clips. You don't want the hatch cover falling on your head or knocking you off the handrail."

I couldn't help picturing that happening, and me tumbling helplessly down into what looked ominously close to my personal nightmare of an unguarded lift shaft. "Keep quiet," I said sharply. "I'm climbing up now and need to concentrate."

I forced my eyes away from the black depths of the downway, gripped the handrail, and launched myself upwards. There was a stab of complaint from my bruised right ankle as I landed, and I teetered wildly from side to side, as unsteady as a thirteen-year-old trying their first ride on the handrail.

I leaned one hand against the wall to steady myself, and reached up with the other. I could easily turn the clips on the bottom edge of the hatch cover, but the top ones were out of my reach. I stretched up as far as I could, so I was brushing the clips with the tips of my fingers, but that got me no closer to being able to turn them.

I groaned and tried the desperation tactic of standing on tiptoe. My right ankle throbbed in protest, but I ignored it. I'd just managed to undo one of the remaining clips, when my right ankle gave way under the strain, and I came horribly close to falling off the handrail.

Resting my back against the coolness of the wall, I took most of my weight on my left foot to let my right ankle recover. Standing on tiptoe obviously stressed my bruised ankle to the limit. If I tried it again, I risked falling, but I couldn't give up when I was so close to releasing Forge.

I decided to compromise by only standing on tiptoe very briefly. I braced myself, went for the last clip, and failed to shift it. I took a minute break before trying and failing again.

The last clip seemed to be stuck firmly in place. I'd have to risk standing on tiptoe longer if I was going to stand any chance of undoing it. I made my third attempt, wincing from the pain in my ankle as I clawed desperately at the clip. I felt like cheering when I felt it move under my fingers, but then the hatch cover came flying off.

I instinctively dodged sideways out of the way, and the cover went bouncing down into the darkness without hitting me, but my abused right ankle inevitably gave way again. I yelped in pain, swayed wildly backwards, recovered once, and then swayed again.

"Amber!"

Forge's voice shouted from above me as I slipped off the handrail. I managed to grab it with my right hand, breaking my fall, and stopping myself from going toppling down to Level 54.

Forge slid out of the hole feet first, lowered himself down with his hands, and dropped neatly onto the steps of the downway. "Amber, are you hurt?"

"I've bruised my right ankle." I tried putting my weight on my right foot. "I think I'm all right so long as I walk carefully."

"Thanks for getting me out of there, Amber. I'm really grateful."

I held out one of the lanterns towards Forge, saw the relieved and delighted expression on his face, and felt a flush of pleasure. "That's all right."

Forge took the lantern and turned to hurry back down the stairs.

"You're going the wrong way," I called after him.

"I just want to put the hatch cover back in place," said Forge.

I found it hard to argue with Forge, but he'd have to climb on the handrail to put the hatch cover back, and it seemed a totally unnecessary risk. "That doesn't matter now."

Forge stooped to pick up the cover. "It does matter. Rescue teams will be using the upways and downways to travel round the Hive. We can't leave the hatch cover lying on the steps where someone could trip over it and get hurt."

I remembered the way I'd put my foot on Linnette's lantern and fallen. "That's true, but we could move it to…"

I let my words trail off because Forge had already jumped up on the handrail. I watched nervously as he put the hatch cover back in place, anticipating a disastrous fall, but Forge was tall enough to reach the clips easily. Within seconds, he was jumping down again. He took off his headband, turned off its lights, and put it in his pocket, then picked up his lantern and came back to join me.

"We should find Linnette now."

"Yes." I led the way up the stairs. "I've been away a very long time, but she's probably still asleep."

"Linnette's asleep? How can she sleep in this dreadful darkness? Especially with a broken leg!"

"I was told to give her two painkilling tablets," I said. "They sent her to sleep."

I could hear Linnette before we reached her. She was making soft snuffling noises in her sleep, but it didn't sound like she was having bad dreams. Forge handed me his lantern and knelt beside her.

"Does she have any injuries other than the broken leg?" he asked.

"I don't think so."

Forge slid his arms carefully under Linnette, and lifted her. I led the way upwards, trying to hold the lanterns so that Forge had as much light as possible. As he lowered Linnette onto the stretcher, I gave a sob of relief.

"We just need to get to the park now, and that should be easy."

"It won't be easy at all." Forge took back his lantern. "We'll need to go most of the way back to our corridor, and then head west and..."

"No, we don't," I interrupted him. "That's the way to the main park entrance, but we can take the shortcut to one of the side entrances. That's only about two corridor lengths north of here."

Forge frowned. "Are you sure you can find the way in this darkness, Amber?"

"I'm certain. Remember that I spend a lot more time in the park than you do. I'll just call Ruby and Atticus to let them know we've found Linnette."

I took out my communicator and pressed the green button. "Hello, Ruby, Atticus, are you there?"

"Yes," Ruby and Atticus answered in unison. "Where are you, Amber?" Atticus continued solo. "We were expecting you to reach the park at least fifteen minutes ago. We were about to call you to ask if you'd got lost."

"I'm not lost. I'm in the shopping area, and I've found both Forge and Linnette, but Linnette's broken her leg. Emergency Services told us to bring Linnette to the park on a stretcher, so we'll be with you soon."

"How can you have found Forge?" Ruby sounded puzzled. "Atticus said he was having treatment in a medical facility."

I hesitated, unsure what to say.

"The medical facility discharged me," said Forge. "I was on my way home when the power went out. I got lost in the dark, but then I heard Amber shouting. We'd better get moving now."

"Good luck," said Ruby.

I put the communicator in my pocket, and collected my backpack and the extra lantern. I found I could hold both lanterns in my left hand, so I grabbed one of the front handles of the stretcher with my right, and started it moving.

Forge took hold of a handle on the other side of the stretcher. "Are you sure this way is north, Amber? I've lost my sense of direction."

I was feeling far more confident now that I was no longer alone with the burden of responsibility for getting Linnette to safety. "I've already done a lot of wandering round this shopping area in the dark, and I'm positive that we turn right from the downway to reach the sandwich bar. We should see it ahead of us in a minute."

"How is your bruised ankle now?" asked Forge.

"My ankle is feeling a lot better, but I can see you're limping. Is your cut leg hurting you?"

Forge stopped limping. "No, it's just a scratch. I can see a clothes stall ahead of us but not a sandwich bar."

"The sandwich bar is just beyond it. Look!" I gestured with my lantern.

"Oh yes." Forge looked nervously round. "I know the peculiar shadows are only the effect of the lanterns swaying, but I saw some odd flashes of light past the sandwich bar."

"Those will just be reflections of our own lanterns." I tugged the stretcher into motion again. "I often buy food at the sandwich bar and go to the park to eat it. Once we reach the sandwich bar, we turn right into a corridor."

Forge was silent until we reached the sandwich bar. "There isn't a corridor here."

"I'd forgotten there was another shop after the sandwich bar." I carried on past the next shop and pointed triumphantly at the corridor on our right. "Now if we go down this corridor, and turn left at the next crossway, we'll reach the park."

As we headed down the corridor, I noticed Forge was limping again. If I asked him about his leg, he'd keep denying he was in pain, and there was no way to avoid him walking to the park. Once we got there, I'd have to make sure both he and Linnette got medical treatment.

Just before we reached the crossway, we found an overturned trolley lying in our path. Its contents, a host of small packages, had scattered across the corridor. I picked up one of the packages, studied it in the light of my lantern, and then tossed it aside.

"Food packs," I said. "Someone from Accommodation Services must have been taking them to restock kitchen units when the lights went out."

We cleared enough packages out of the way to tow the stretcher through. "Are you sure we turn left at the crossway?" asked Forge.

"Yes." We reached the crossway, and I laughed and pointed. "See for yourself."

"You're right," cried Forge. "I can see a light in the distance!"

We headed eagerly down the corridor. As we got closer, I could see it wasn't just one light ahead of us, but two glowing lanterns, one on either side of the park door.

I didn't notice the shadowy figure sitting on the floor between the lanterns until he got to his feet, picked up one of the lanterns, and came to meet us. It was Atticus.

CHAPTER TWENTY-TWO

"I'm deeply relieved to see you, Amber," said Atticus. "How is Linnette?"

"I was told to give her two painkillers," I said, "and those sent her to sleep. I'm hoping that's a good sign."

Atticus nodded, turned to Forge, and waved a reproving finger at him. "As for you... Well, I'll have to save telling you what I think of your behaviour until we're alone, because I'm planning to use extreme language. I've no idea how Amber managed to get you out of the vent system, but I do know that you didn't deserve her efforts."

Forge sighed. "I know I didn't. You can shout at me all you like later on, Atticus, but we need to get medical help for Linnette now."

"Forge needs medical help too," I said.

"No, I don't," said Forge.

I wouldn't normally argue with Forge, but I was worried about his injury. "You *do* need medical help. You've been limping all the way here."

Atticus stooped to peer at Forge's leg. "There's a lot of blood where something cut through your leggings and into your calf. Let me roll up the material to see how badly you've hurt yourself."

Forge took a rapid step backwards. "There's no need for you to look at my leg, Atticus. It's only a scratch."

"It's bleeding an awful lot for something that's only a scratch," said Atticus.

"My leg stopped bleeding ages ago," said Forge.

"It's possible that it stopped bleeding at some point," said Atticus, "but I can assure you it's started again now. You're dripping blood all over the floor. You must have opened up the wound walking here."

He straightened up again. "Amber's right. You need a doctor to treat that leg."

Forge groaned. "If I go for treatment, the medical staff will ask lots of questions about how I injured myself. I can't tell them the truth, and if they spot that I'm lying then we'll all get into trouble."

"If you tell the medical staff that you fell and cut yourself, they won't bother asking any more questions," said Atticus. "They've already had to treat dozens of people who've had accidents in the dark."

Atticus held open the park door. I helped Forge to steer Linnette's stretcher inside, then stopped, stunned by the sight of the park. I'd expected the lights to be on a brighter version of the moon and stars setting. I'd expected the park to be filled with people carrying lanterns. I hadn't expected everyone to be crowded on to the event lawn, and dancing to Carnival music.

"What's going on?" I asked. "How did an emergency evacuation turn into a Carnival party?"

Atticus laughed. "This is all Shanna's doing. When we arrived in the park, most of the teens in our area were already here, and they were all frightened and upset. Shanna tracked down the park keeper, told him she'd brought along her data cube of Carnival party music, and talked him into turning on the park event sound system. Fifteen minutes later, she had everyone happily dancing."

The music ended, and the dancers turned to look expectantly at where Shanna stood on the circular event stage. Shanna had her blonde hair falling loose around her shoulders, she was wearing a spectacular silver Carnival dress, and was surrounded by a ring of lanterns. The dress confused me. Had Shanna really chosen to pack her Carnival dress in her emergency bag? I supposed that she must have done.

Shanna's voice boomed over the park event sound system. "Next we've got a song that's a personal favourite of mine. It's Blue Zone's very own Pasquale, performing his latest hit song that he wrote himself."

There was a cascade of rippling music, and a male voice started singing.

"*We met at Carnival.*"

Shanna waved at the crowd, like someone conducting an orchestra, and they all joined in the singing.

"*Her mask was silver and her hair was gold.*"

I exchanged dazed looks with Forge. "She's amazing," he said proudly. "Absolutely amazing."

Atticus shrugged. "Shanna was distinctly unhelpful when the power first went out, but I have to admit that she's doing a wonderful job entertaining everyone now."

He grabbed a handle of the stretcher and started towing it along the path. "The staff from our local medical facility have set up a treatment area over this way."

Forge and I followed Atticus along the path, through some trees, to a smaller grassy area surrounded by flowerbeds. Giant lanterns illuminated a large array of stretchers, a gazebo shrouded with sheets, and a crowd of people sitting on chairs or the grass. I noticed that several of them were swaying in time to the distant music.

A uniformed woman hurried over to meet us, her eyes on Linnette's stretcher. "I'm the acting triage doctor. What happened?"

"Linnette fell on the downway," I said. "We think she's broken her leg."

The woman glanced at her dataview. "Is this the Linnette 2514-1003-947 that we were expecting?"

"That's right. She was in a lot of pain. I was told to give her the two tablets from this packet and they sent her to sleep."

I handed over the empty packet. The woman studied it briefly. "Thank you. We'll take care of her now."

She waved her arm, and a man hurried over to take charge of Linnette's stretcher. "This is Linnette 2514-1003-947," said the doctor. "She goes straight to the top of the queue."

The man nodded. "The park keeper just arrived. He says he'd like to let the music go on until midnight to wear all the teens out, before trying to get them to go to sleep. He wants to know if that's all right with us."

"I think that's a good idea. We want people sleeping soundly rather than having nightmares, and it will take us until well past midnight to catch up with treating the incoming casualties anyway, so..."

At this point, Pasquale hit the climax of his song. Not that you could hear him at all, since the crowd on the event lawn drowned him out with their own wildly enthusiastic singing.

"*Blue Zone girl!*"

A dozen of the waiting patients joined in with the repeat of the line. "*Blue Zone girl!*"

The doctor turned to face the singers with a forbidding frown, but then muttered to herself. "Better to have them noisy and happy than quiet and scared."

She turned back to us again, and I hastily spoke. "There's Forge too. He..."

I saw Forge giving me a forbidding look, and broke off my sentence.

"Yes?" prompted the doctor.

"Forge was very helpful," I said lamely.

Atticus sighed. "Forge has cut his leg and it's dripping blood. He claims it's only a scratch, but he'd say that even if he was cut to the bone."

The doctor pointed at a chair. "Please sit down, Forge, and I'll assess your leg injury."

Forge glared at Atticus, and reluctantly sat down. The woman cautiously peeled back the blood-stained fabric covering his calf, and I winced as I saw the size of the gash in his leg.

The woman shook her head. "Forge, you'll need to stay with us until someone is free to treat your leg."

"I don't need treatment."

The doctor's voice developed an edge of sarcasm. "Are you imprinted with medical knowledge, Forge?"

"No, but..."

"Well, I am, and I assure you that this injury does require treatment. What is your identity code?"

Forge was still battling the inevitable. "But it's just a scratch."

"His identity code is 2514-0253-884," said Atticus helpfully. "We'll leave both Forge and Linnette in your excellent care now."

Atticus turned and walked back along the path. I gave a last wary look at Forge's face, before hurrying to catch up with Atticus.

"Forge is annoyed with you," I said anxiously.

"I don't care," said Atticus.

"He's probably annoyed with me too."

"We had to make sure he got medical treatment, Amber. Did you see the state of his leg?"

I couldn't help picturing the gash in Forge's leg, and winced again. "Yes."

"Now let's find the others from our corridor, and tell them you've brought Linnette here. They're all very worried about the two of you." Atticus paused for a second. "Well, I doubt Reece cares about anything except the fact he's in trouble. He's lucky that Ruby has him under guard, because if I was in charge of him…"

Atticus realized I'd stopped moving and turned to come back to me. "Is something…?"

"Hush!" I interrupted him. "Listen!"

Atticus gave me a puzzled look. "Listen to what?"

"I thought I heard someone crying. Yes, there it is again."

"I can only hear Shanna's party music."

"It's coming from this way." I headed into the trees and stared around. It was so dark that I almost missed seeing the huddled shape at the foot of a dwarf oak tree. I went over to kneel next to it. "Are you all right?"

The shape lifted its head, and I saw it was a girl. Her face was blotchy from crying, but looked vaguely familiar.

"You're Celeste from corridor 19, aren't you?" Atticus came to kneel beside me.

The girl nodded.

"How did you get here?" asked Atticus. "I thought all the

eighteen-year-olds were at a Lottery candidates' event in a different area."

"Oh yes," Celeste's voice was suddenly loud with anger. "We were all at the Lottery candidates' event to celebrate the end of our time on Teen Level. I was supposed to celebrate the fact I was about to say goodbye to all my friends and never see them again. I was supposed to celebrate the fact I was about to say goodbye to the boy I loved and never see him again either."

I didn't know what I could say to comfort her.

"Counsellors have been lecturing us for weeks," Celeste's voice abruptly changed from anger to bitter despair. "On the day after Carnival, we'll enter Lottery. We'll be assessed, optimized, allocated, and imprinted. We'll be given our levels and sent out as proudly productive adult members of the Hive, but becoming an adult means we have to end our teen relationships."

"It has to be that way," said Atticus sadly. "Everyone will come out of Lottery as different levels, so..."

"I know!" Celeste snapped at him. "They kept saying that over and over again. Once people are ten, twenty, or fifty levels apart, then old friendships become embarrassing to both parties, and the closest of relationships disintegrate under the strain. The counsellors told us that it was better to make a clean break before Lottery, and walk away with the happy memories of Teen Level intact, but making a clean break from the most important person in your life is like..."

"Like losing part of yourself," I finished the sentence for her.

"Exactly. You understand why I couldn't do it. I told Seb that we should stay together whatever our levels after Lottery, but he..."

Her face crumpled, and I finished the sentence again. "He wanted to split up?"

Celeste rubbed her face with the back of her hand. "Yes. Seb said that I was being ridiculous. He told me that we had to follow Hive tradition, and say goodbye on the last day of Carnival. When I kept arguing with him, he started shouting that he was obviously going to come out of Lottery far higher than me, and wouldn't want a low level ex-girlfriend trying to cling on to him."

She lifted her head defiantly. "So then I told him that he could go waste himself, and I walked out of the event. I was nearly home, just transferring from the express belt to the medium belt, when the lights went out and the belts stopped moving."

I caught my breath. I'd imagined people trapped in lifts in the darkness. I'd imagined people falling when the moving stairs stopped. I hadn't thought about what would happen to those riding the belt system, especially the express belt. "Were many people hurt when the belts suddenly stopped moving?"

"They didn't stop suddenly," said Celeste. "They just gradually slowed down."

"There's an inertial braking system that brings the belts to a controlled halt in emergencies," said Atticus. "Our warden training course included an explanation about how that works, but I didn't understand a word of it."

"Anyway, only a few people fell," said Celeste, "but everyone was panicking in the darkness until some people with lanterns arrived. They took us to the shopping area, and then we moved on to the park."

She groaned. "I wish I'd never suggested staying with Seb after Lottery. Now my last memory of him is going to be the superior pitying expression on his face when he said he was going to be much higher level than me."

"Lottery is unpredictable," I said. "You could be the one that ends up higher level."

"I hope I do," said Celeste savagely. "I hope I end up fifty levels higher than Seb. I hope I end up elite while Seb is a Level 99 Sewage Technician!"

She got to her feet. "It was good of you to check that I'm all right, but now I'm going to join in the party. Seb isn't the only boy in the world."

Atticus and I stood up as well, and watched her head off towards the event area. "It's probably better for Celeste to be angry than hurt," I said.

"Perhaps," said Atticus, "but I pity any boy who tries dancing with her in her current mood."

There was a long moment of silence. I was thinking about Celeste's situation. Next year, Atticus and I would be entering Lottery. Did I really want to get into a relationship that could only last twelve months before ending in a painful breakup? I wasn't sure that I did.

I tried to work out how to say that to Atticus, but he said it first. "It may not be a good idea for us to get involved with each other. A year from now..."

"I agree. We'd be constantly counting down the time until we have to split up."

"It's not that I don't like you, Amber," said Atticus. "It's that I think I could like you far too much."

I nodded.

"I'd still like us to be partners for Carnival though," he added. "Just as friends who aren't going to move on to anything serious."

"I'd like that too."

We walked on to the event area. "The others are over by that tree," Atticus said.

There was a ring of trees around the edge of the event area. I was about to ask which tree he meant, when I spotted a cluster of familiar figures. We dodged our way through the crowd to join them.

"Amber's here," Atticus yelled above the sound of the music.

They all turned to look at us. "Amber!" several voices chorused my name at once, and I was hugged by Margot and Preeja.

"Did you find Linnette?" Preeja asked anxiously.

"Yes. I'm afraid she's broken her leg, so she's over in the medical area. Forge is there too, getting treatment for his cut leg."

"How did Forge get here?" asked Margot.

I remembered the story that Forge had told Ruby. "The medical facility discharged Forge, and he was on his way home when the power went out. I met him when I was searching for Linnette."

"But if Forge has already had his cut leg treated once, why does he need it treating again?" asked Preeja.

"He fell in the dark and reopened the wound." I hastily changed the subject. "I can't see Casper. Where is he?"

"He's down the other end of the park by the lake," said Margot.

"What? Why?"

"Most of the park animals and birds have moved down that end of the park to get away from the crowds and the noise, so the feeding stations there are very busy," said Preeja. "The park volunteers are helping to keep them stocked with food, and Casper is in charge of feeding station 14."

I frowned. "Yes, the poor park animals and birds must find this very confusing."

"Don't waste your sympathy on them," said Margot. "They're used to moving out of the way of park events, and Casper told us the park has enough animal and bird food stored to last them weeks. We're the ones stuck with surviving on disgusting emergency ration bars. You should organize things better, Atticus."

"It's not my fault," said Atticus.

"Yes, it is," said Margot. "You're our emergency warden."

Shanna's voice came over the event sound system, announcing another song by Pasquale, and Atticus turned to face me. "Would you like to dance, Amber?"

"Yes, I would."

Atticus took my hand, and we ran to join the crowd of dancers before Margot could start complaining again.

"I've just remembered something," I said. "On our way to the park, Forge and I passed an overturned trolley of food packs for kitchen units. If I went back and salvaged them, they might be edible. At least, more edible than the ration bars."

"Oh no!" said Atticus firmly. "You've rescued Linnette. You've rescued Forge. You aren't going wandering off again to rescue a heap of food packs. Margot can either eat the ration bars or beg bird food from Casper."

I laughed.

CHAPTER TWENTY-THREE

Two days later, Linnette arrived at the event area, with Forge pushing her in a manual wheelchair. Reece was still under arrest somewhere, and Shanna was in the middle of her third marathon session of party music, but all the rest of our corridor group gathered round Linnette to welcome her back. She was just explaining how she'd fallen on the downway, when the lights in the park ceiling suddenly flared from moon to full sun brightness.

Everyone shaded dazzled eyes with their hands, and cheered wildly. The music abruptly stopped, and a new tune started, the changeover so fast that Shanna had obviously prepared this in advance.

"The suns were shining in the park."

The girl singing was rated Level 1 like Pasquale, but she'd only come out of Lottery the previous year, so this was her first song that had gained much attention. Some of the crowd knew it, others clearly didn't, but by the second chorus they'd all got the hang of the tune and words and were singing along.

"The suns were shining in the park."

Once the song ended, there was a crackle on the sound system, and a faintly embarrassed male voice spoke. "Attention everyone. Blue Zone now has power, but Emergency Services are requesting that everyone stays in the parks for now. Maintenance teams need to get all the upways, downways, and lifts back in action, and hasties have to check the corridors for hazards. They estimate that will take about four hours."

The crowd booed.

"It's no use complaining at me," said the male voice. "I'm only the park keeper. The good news is that Blue Zone's main freight transport links are already back in operation, and will be bringing in stockpiles of supplies from Turquoise and Navy Zones. We should be receiving a consignment of food and drink within the next two hours."

There was another crackle and Shanna spoke. "You heard him, everyone. Free food and drink is on the way, and this is going to be real food not emergency ration bars!"

The music started up again and we all yelled the lyrics.

"The suns were shining in the park."

Forge came to stand next to me, and stooped to shout in my ear. "I've just got to go and..."

The rest of his words were drowned out by the next line of the song, and he hurried off. I assumed that he'd gone to join Shanna.

About an hour later, the crates of food and drink arrived. The people delivering them barely had time to take off the lids before they were mobbed by desperate teens who'd been surviving on water and emergency ration bars for two days.

Half of our corridor group joined the charge for the crates, but I didn't have the build to fight my way through the crush, so I stood watching their progress with Linnette and Casper. My mind was fully occupied with the prospect of getting decent food at last, so I didn't notice the music had stopped until Shanna arrived to join us.

"Where is Forge?" she asked.

I frowned. "I haven't seen him since just after the power came back on. I thought he was with you."

At that moment, the warriors of our corridor group returned in triumph with a crate that they tipped out on the grass.

"They've sent us masses of luxury food and drink!" I rejoiced.

"We deserve it after being starved for days," said Margot.

"Melon juice, Violet Zone cheese, and Turquoise Zone blueberry crunch cakes!" I dropped to my knees to grab at the bounty. "What would you like, Linnette?"

"Anything will do," said Linnette, "so long as it isn't a ration bar."

I put a random set of food packs and bottles on her lap, and saw Casper was standing looking doubtfully down at the assortment of food and drink. "Would you like to try some melon juice, Casper?"

"I want orange juice and the Blue Zone cheese with holes in it."

"Melon juice tastes wonderful," I coaxed. "So does Violet Zone cheese."

Casper shook his head. "My budget says that I have orange juice and Blue Zone cheese for lunch today. Madeleine from Support Services runs my learning support group. She worked out my budget with me, and she's says it's important that I stick to it."

"We don't have to pay for these things, Casper," said Shanna.

Casper still looked doubtful. "Reece told me something was free once when it wasn't. We should check with someone official."

Shanna looked irritated, and opened her mouth to say something, but a voice spoke from behind me. "The food and drink is definitely free."

I knew that voice. It was Buzz! I turned round, and was confused to see she was wearing the red and blue, diagonal striped uniform of Emergency Services.

"Casper, this is like one of the Carnival events that have free food and drink," she added.

Casper nodded, and smiled happily as he picked out a food pack for himself.

"What are you doing here, Buzz," I asked, "and why are you wearing those clothes?"

"I chose to wear an Emergency Services uniform to reassure the people we were rescuing from lifts. Now the power is back on, there are a terrifyingly large number of Blue Zone teens that need a psychologist to assess their actions during the power outage and decide on appropriate treatment. I was automatically assigned all the ones in this area, because you're still on my case list."

"What? But I haven't done anything wrong. It was Reece who frightened everyone, not me."

Buzz laughed. "I didn't say you'd done anything wrong, Amber. I said that you were still on my case list. The behaviour monitoring alert on you is still active, and has flagged you for multiple actions requiring my attention. I'm curious why you froze in terror on a cliff, but volunteered to wander round in the darkness searching for a lost girl."

I shrugged. "I'm scared of heights, but I'm not scared of the dark."

"That's intriguing given Hive culture encourages a fear of darkness and the Outside." Buzz sighed. "I wish I could discuss it further with you, but sadly I'm going to be far too busy with all my other cases. I came to see you first, because I hoped I'd be able to deal with your case extremely quickly. You're uninjured and showing no visible signs of trauma, so I'll sign you off and leave you to enjoy your meal in peace."

There was a chime from Buzz's pocket. She took out her dataview, checked it, and groaned. "A hasty just arrested yet another problem teen and is bringing him in for... Oh, there they are!"

She waved an arm, and I saw a female hasty coming towards us. I blinked as I saw who she had with her.

"Forge!" Shanna, Atticus, and I chorused his name in unison.

Buzz gave me an amused look. "This is your friend, Forge? The one who rescued you from the cliff?"

"Yes, why has he been arrested?"

"Because a maintenance team caught him crawling through the vent system." Buzz frowned at the display on her dataview.

I exchanged bemused glances with Atticus. Shanna was glaring at the approaching Forge, and he gave her a nervous look, but neither of them had the chance to say anything before the hasty started talking.

"This is Forge 2514-0253-884. What would you like me to do with him?"

Buzz looked up, studied Forge briefly, and then gave an abrupt nod. "We're too busy dealing with cases who are a danger to others, to waste much time on a boy addicted to taking risks. We'll settle for putting a tracking bracelet on him for a month."

"What?" Forge looked appalled. "A tracking bracelet like the ones that little children wear? You can't do that to me!"

Buzz grinned at him. "I think we can. You won't be able to go anywhere you shouldn't without setting off alarms. Hopefully that will encourage you to keep out of trouble in future."

The hasty produced a bracelet from her pocket, and took hold of Forge's arm. "I suggest you keep still and accept the inevitable, because any argument will just end in you wearing the bracelet for longer."

Forge cringed with embarrassment as the tracking bracelet was fixed around his wrist.

The others had been watching this in silence, but now Margot spoke in a bitter voice. "I hope you'll give Reece a much bigger punishment than making him wear a tracking bracelet. He terrified everyone. It's his fault that Linnette broke her leg."

"My job isn't to punish anyone's past actions, but to make sure their future behaviour is beneficial to the Hive," said Buzz.

"So you'll let Reece carry on without any penalty at all? What if he hurts someone again? What if he hurts Linnette again?" Margot put a protective hand on Linnette's shoulder.

"Reece will be given corrective treatment to ensure that does not happen," said Buzz gently. "Treatment is always more constructive than punishment, however Reece's disruptive personality traits are likely to have a harmful impact on his Lottery result."

"Disruptive," Margot repeated the word eagerly. "You mean Lottery will make him low level?"

"It's impossible to predict the outcome of a process as complex as Lottery," said Buzz, "but Reece does not have the cooperative, conformist nature that is required for most positions in the Hive."

"Good," said Margot. "I hope Reece comes out of Lottery as a Level 99 Sewage Technician."

Buzz laughed. "Perhaps he will. Goodbye now." She turned and walked off with the hasty.

Forge gave a despairing groan. "If I have to wear this bracelet for a month, that means I'll be wearing it during the next two swimming competitions. The other teams will make my life a misery."

"Never mind your swimming competitions." Shanna spat the words at him. "What about the Carnival parties? I'm going to look ridiculous dancing with you when you're wearing a child's tracking bracelet."

She turned and stormed off.

Forge started moving after her, but then stopped. "I expect she'll need a few hours to calm down."

"I expect she'll need a few weeks to calm down, and I can't blame her for that," said Atticus. "What were you doing in the vent system, Forge? You'd been stuck in there for days. Amber had to rescue you. Why go back in there again?"

"When Amber let me out of the vent system, I was so busy worrying about how we'd get Linnette to the park that I left my backpack behind. I didn't remember it until I was having my leg treated by the medical staff. When the power came back on, I thought I could run back and retrieve it before there were any people around to see me."

Atticus shook his head in disbelief. "What was inside the backpack that was so important?"

"It wasn't what was inside the backpack," said Forge. "It was the fact the backpack had my name written on it. I was worried that someone would find it and I'd get into trouble. Unfortunately, there was a maintenance team checking the downway, and they spotted me climbing out of the inspection hatch."

Atticus sighed. "Maybe it's a good thing that you were caught. Having to wear that bracelet will teach you not to take silly risks in future."

I didn't say a word. I didn't believe that having to wear a child's tracking bracelet for a month would be enough to cure Forge of taking risks. As soon as it was removed, he'd be asking me to let him use the inspection hatch in my room to go exploring the vent system again. Even worse, I'd probably find myself agreeing to let him do it.

CHAPTER TWENTY-FOUR

On the morning after Carnival, I walked to the nearest major transport corridor. It was vastly wider than any normal corridor, with slow, medium, and express belts running side-by-side. I didn't step on to the belts myself, just went to stand with my back against the corridor wall.

There were only a couple of other teens there when I arrived, but gradually more of us arrived, until we formed a solid line along the corridor wall. We ranged in age from the fourteen-year-olds who had arrived on Teen Level just under a year ago, to the seventeen-year-olds like me.

We didn't talk to each other, just patiently waited, our eyes on the belts. They'd normally be filled with passengers at this time of the morning, but today they were completely empty. I wasn't sure why the custom had started, whether it was out of respect or superstition, but no younger teens ever rode the belt system on the first day of Lottery.

I'd been standing there for fifteen minutes, when I saw the first figure go by on the express belt. It was a girl with long black hair trailing down her back. She was followed by a second girl, a boy, and then a whole succession of different figures. All eighteen years old, all sitting on a bag, all with tense, distracted faces, they seemed totally unaware of the rest of us standing there watching them.

In previous years, I'd watched the eighteen-year-olds travelling to their Lottery test centres, and happily daydreamed of the day when I'd be heading to Lottery myself. I'd pictured myself being allocated my Hive level and occupation, being imprinted with all the knowledge I'd need to do my work, and starting my adult life. In those dreams, I was always high level, successful, triumphant.

Now everything was different. I was burningly aware that next year I'd be riding the belt system to a Lottery test centre myself. I was no longer picturing myself leaving Lottery and heading up the Hive in triumph. Since my trip to the medical facility on Level 93, I'd given up daydreams, and accepted the harsh reality. I wouldn't be heading up the Hive but down.

I stood there for what seemed like hours, watching the eighteen-year-olds go by, and wondering what they were thinking. Finally, the express belt was empty. The candidates had all reached their assessment centres, and were beginning the test process that would decide their futures.

One by one, the teens around me turned and walked away, but I stood there alone, still watching the empty belt go past me. I was resigned to the fact that Lottery would definitely send me down the Hive. The important questions were exactly how far down, and what task it would assign me.

A year from now, I'd learn the answers to those questions. The mystery of my reaction to Forge would no longer matter, because I'd never see him or any of my other friends again. I would be starting a new life as an adult, but would I still be the same person after Lottery? Would I still be the untidy Amber who was scared of heights, or would having information imprinted on my brain change me forever?

I hadn't been scared of the darkness during the power outage, but I did fear the terrifying black unknown that was my future. No lantern could help me see what lay ahead for me. The Lottery of 2532, unpredictable, merciless, implacable, would decide my destiny. I would be assessed, optimized, allocated and imprinted along with a million others.

Some new figures came into view on the express belt. The eighteen-year-olds were all in assessment centres, and none of us younger teens would ride the belt system today, but these were adults not teens. Four people in the blue uniforms of hasties, and the ominous grey-clad figure of a nosy.

I hastily turned and walked away. There was no way for me to avoid the judgement of Lottery, no way for me to appeal against its verdict, no way for me to avoid being imprinted. I just had to hope that the words I'd been taught all my life were true, and the Hive really did know best.

Message From Janet Edwards

Thank you for reading Perilous. This book is a prequel novella in the Hive Mind series, and Amber's story continues in the first full-length book, Telepath.

You may also be interested in my books set in the very different Portal Future universe, where humanity portals between hundreds of different colony worlds scattered across space. These books include the Earth Girl trilogy, the Exodus series, and related stories.

Please visit my website, www.janetedwards.com, to see the current list of my books. You can also make sure you don't miss future books by signing up to get an email alert when there's a new release.

I'd like to thank Andrew Angel and Juliet for Beta reading Perilous. Any remaining problems are entirely my fault.

                    Best wishes from Janet Edwards

Printed in Poland
by Amazon Fulfillment
Poland Sp. z o.o., Wrocław